Eldon Moran

Short-Hand Made Easy

Eldon Moran

Short-Hand Made Easy

ISBN/EAN: 9783337390198

Printed in Europe, USA, Canada, Australia, Japan

Cover: Foto ©Andreas Hilbeck / pixelio.de

More available books at **www.hansebooks.com**

SHORT-HAND MADE EASY.

Rapid Writing Simplified.   The Reporting Style of the
American Pitman System Clearly Taught.   A
Series of Lessons prepared specially
for Self-Instruction and
Home Study.

BY ELDON MORAN,

*President Central College of Short-hand, Author of the
"Reporting Style," the Sign Book, the Short-hand
Primer, Correspondence Manual, etc.*

To give this book an increased practical value to the student, the Publishers have engaged the Author to
give two individual lessons by mail to
each purchaser. Lesson cou-
pons are printed on
page 63.

NEW YORK:
W. N. SWETT & CO., PUBLISHERS,
28 READE STREET.
1891.

THE PITMAN SYSTEM.

Persons not informed think there are scores of systems of short-hand in common use — about as many different systems as reporters, some suppose. This is a great mistake. In Germany there are but two in common use; only about three in France, and in America not more than half a dozen worthy of notice. There are, of course, more than six authors — perhaps two dozen. They are teachers, not inventors. A great majority of them advocate the Pitman system. We hear of the systems of Longley, Munson, Burnz, Scott-Browne, Graham and others. They are all Pitman, however, and the distinction in name is made for convenience mainly. These writers differ in detail, and that is about all. It would not be seriously claimed that they are the originators of the system they present.

To be broadly capable, readily acquired and easily remembered, a short-hand system must be scientific — not merely expeditious. A collection of arbitrary expedients, if sufficiently large, may serve for reproducing ordinary discourse; but the inventiveness of the reporter, or the old cumbersome long-hand, must be resorted to when newly coined words, unusual proper names, technical terms or provincialisms are encountered. A system, to be scientific, must have a basis of principal; be so related to known sciences as to be quickly apprehended; so facile as to be equal to any emergency of speed, dialect, borrowed words or foreign names or accent. The Pitman phonography meets these requirements. No matter what changes the language may undergo, it will be impossible for it to extend beyond the capabilities of this far-reaching system. It is adapted, first of all, to the human voice in general and, incidentally, to the English language in particular.

PUBLISHERS' PREFACE.

To-day thousands of young men and women are pursuing the study of Short-hand. Hundreds of thousands would do so if they had the opportunity.

This book offers a most excellent opportunity to the large and increasing number of deserving young people who wish to learn the art of swift writing.

This book is exactly suited to self-instruction.

It was prepared by one of the swiftest Stenographers and most expert teachers in America. Professor Moran, the author, was Court Reporter for eight years, serving a portion of this time in Judge Gresham's Court, and reporting cases for Vice-President Hendricks, General Ben. Harrison, Senator Voorhees and other prominent lawyers.

He taught Short-hand with great success for seven years at the University of Iowa, and has perhaps given instructions in Short-hand to more persons than any other living teacher. The books of which he is the author are used in hundreds of colleges and high schools.

This little work has been prepared with great care, and we confidently believe that any intelligent student can obtain a thorough knowledge of all the essential principles of the Pitman System by an honest study of its pages.

Every beginner is earnestly recommended to avail himself of the lessons by mail to which the coupons at the back of the book entitle him. A certain amount of individual instruction just at the outset is of very great importance to the student just starting. If you will only begin right, you will avoid mistakes that might otherwise prove serious.

The author also agrees to send to each learner Cards of Introduction to other students of Short-hand, with whom he may carry on a correspondence, making use of characters to some extent. Letter-writing in Short-hand is a great benefit to the person who studies at home, and it is as helpful as it is interesting.

The foolish notion once prevailed, that only a genius could learn Short-hand. The old text-books published twenty years ago were difficult to learn from. A book that is easy and simple, like this one, which is an outcome from the many years experience of a practical teacher, will enable the intelligent, earnest student to accomplish wonders. To every ambitious young man and young woman we say, Take this book and study it faithfully an hour more or less every day, and you will find stenography as easy to understand as it is useful in business and beautiful in theory.

New York City, January, 1892.

OUTLOOK.

The value of stenographic writing as an accomplishment, and as a part of a practical business education, is so obvious, and the proofs of its utility so various and satisfactory, that the demand for a knowledge of the art is spreading with an increased rapidity. The pursuit of stenography as a distinct calling has grown beyond all expectation. Already, in each of the older states and principal cities, the number of those engaged in the short-hand writing business reaches into thousands. The work is pleasant, instructive, and profitable. Will it remain so? We will notice a fact which, in many minds, is the occasion for anxiety as to the future—the increasing number of students. But it should be borne in mind that a large, perhaps the larger, part of learners wish stenography as an accomplishment. Besides, thousands of young men every year resign their positions as stenographers to enter some profession or commercial enterprise. Fully as many young women, also, reluctantly though it may be, annually give up short-hand for the more tranquil life in a home of their own. Other natural causes also keep thinning the ranks. On the other hand, and for various reasons not necessary to enumerate, the demand for a greater number of stenographers continually increases. We know of nothing likely to check this demand, while certain events, likely to come to pass, as, for example, the perfection of long-line telephones, would almost double the amount of stenographic work to be done. When the knowledge of short-hand shall have become universal, the stenographic profession will still exist; just as book-keepers would still be needed, although every one understood arithmetic and the science of accounts. So important has short-hand become, that the time approaches when a knowledge of it will be considered an indispensable part of a business education.

INTRODUCTION.

The aim of this work is to present the Pitman system in the concrete — not merely in the abstract; to teach the *how* of short-hand, rather than the *why* of it.

The method of instruction employed is practical and progressive. The principles are taken up and explained in an orderly manner, and the student directed how to apply them correctly in the work of forming the characters rapidly and artistically. Two or three new principles only are introduced in a single lesson, and a list of words inserted which are to be written in accordance therewith. The words chosen for this purpose are those in common use. The drill which enables the learner to write and read them with the required speed, fixes the characters firmly in his memory. No word or phrase is introduced until the learner has been fully directed how to write it in the proper manner. The student who, taking the lessons in turn, masters each, will, upon completing the course, be a competent writer of short-hand.

In Lesson 1, will be found a key and explanation of the short-hand characters given in the accompanying plate. Compare your work frequently with the engraved characters. Write a small hand; place your words closely together, speaking them aloud as you write them. Occasionally read over what you have written. Three important rules are: 1, practice; 2, practice; 3, practice! All beginners write too large. You probably do. Your characters should be but little, if any, longer than those shown in the lesson. Some practice with a pencil is useful, but a pen should be used mostly.

WHAT TO DO.

1. Always write on ruled paper, and hold your pen in a nearly upright position.

2. Send a copy of plate 1 to the author, at St. Louis, for correction.

3. Use good black ink, and whatever pen you find most satisfactory.

4. Read over at least once everything you write.

5. Practice *every* day without fail, if only for a few minutes.

6. Practice on no matter not found in your lessons.

7. Write a *good deal* from dictation; that is, exercises as they are read aloud to you. If possible, get a fellow-student; dictate by turns and criticise each other's work.

8. Occasionally read over an exercise written a week previously.

9. Each exercise should be written *slowly at first*, gradually increasing the speed afterwards.

10. Learn each word *well*, for it is always expressed by the same character in actual reporting.

11. Form the habit of phrasing, or joining words together.

12. Write small; remember the standard, one-sixth of an inch.

13. Hold your note book firmly by placing your left thumb and finger two inches above the base line.

14. Always carry some short-hand matter with you to study spare moments.

15. Whenever proper in writing, employ the characters you have learned.

16. Corresponding with other short-hand students is earnestly recommended.

17. When this course of lessons has been learned, the student's practice need not be limited to the exercises here given, but easy newspaper articles, the prose part of school readers, printed collections of business letters, and published reports of law and convention proceedings may be profitably used for this purpose. Great care should be taken to write each article properly the first time, and to re-write it afterwards not less than half a dozen times with gradually increased speed. Those students who study short-hand with the view of making it profitable in business, would do well to provide themselves with a copy of the "Reporting Style," a book for professional stenographers. The price of this book is $1.50. Sample pages are sent free. Address, Central College of Correspondence, St. Louis, Mo.

ADVICE TO THE STUDENT.

BY THE AUTHOR.

Would you like to be able to write short-hand? Certainly. Short-hand will pay you; besides, if you do not learn it, you will, by-and-by, be considered behind the times. A knowledge of this art cannot be picked up in the street. It will take a little *work*, but of course you have patience and grit. You would like the assistance of a kind and skillful teacher? But if you have none, perhaps you will allow *me* to be your instructor? I will not forget that you are just beginning, and that you need every point made as clear and plain as possible. Yes, certainly, I can teach you, and I have no doubt you will work faithfully, and have this wonderful art of swift writing well learned in just a few months. I feel quite sure I can help you over all the hard places, for I have taught many, yes, *very* many, young persons of your age. And, to be honest, I must say, too, that there are some persons of your age, and some still older, that I do not like to teach — I would really rather not. Why? Because they do not treat their teacher just right. They agree to work at short-hand *every day*, a *little*, any way. Then after a while, without any good excuse, they skip a day, and that causes trouble. By-and-by they skip another day; then next they miss two days. Instead of copying each lesson ten times, *or more*, they write it nine times, then eight, then seven, and at last only once. Of course they do poorly and get discouraged. They fail to become rapid short-hand writers, and the teacher gets the blame.

Now it would be an unnecessary expense for you to come where I am and have me teach you from a blackboard. Still I will be your teacher, and you will be my pupil, if you will only follow the directions which I give here. But *I am not willing* to teach you, unless you firmly resolve *now*, before proceeding further, that you will *do your part* as an earnest student. If you are not willing to do this, then I say, drop short-hand right now, and never touch it again.

Short-hand is a grand accomplishment, and you ought not merely to play with it. I trust you are seriously in earnest. If you are, I will take pleasure in proving my interest in your welfare by writing you a personal letter in short-hand characters as soon as you have finished the sixth lesson. You will then well deserve a word of encouragement from me. You should write me first, giving information as to your age, occupation, how much time you study each day, who, if any one, you have for a class-mate, etc. Address me at St. Louis. You may, if you wish, send a copy of plate 1 for me to examine. Also, would you like to have me send you a card introducing you to two or three other persons of your own age, with whom you may correspond in characters? This will be pleasant, and those who are learning can help each other a great deal in this way.

It may be your intention to learn, not *now*, but at some "more favorable time" in the future. To you who are disposed to procrastinate, that "more favorable time" will never arrive! You may as well write it down, *now or never!*

The younger you begin, the more certain you will be of succeeding. If you are under middle age, have good sight and hearing, the use of your hands, some little education, and a spark of ambition, then you can afford to devote the time necessary to acquire this art. Once more, however, I say before beginning these lessons, make up your mind that you are going to *master them*, or let them alone entirely.

ST. LOUIS, MO., Feb. 1892.

WRITING BY SOUND.

No attention is paid to spelling; words are written the easiest way possible. Silent letters are omitted, as *e* in *yoke*. To illustrate, read this sentence to some friend: *That larg felo lookt hi and lo for the lime kil on the naro ej ov the hil.* He would get your meaning just the same, no matter how the words were spelled.

At first, copy the characters slowly and carefully; continue doing so until you can write them correctly. The young like to practice, but the grown persons execute better. The young like writing; the old like study. Short-hand requires little study but much practice; hence the young succeed the best. Short-hand is something to be *done*, not merely *thought about*. It requires the *hand* more than the *head*. The small dots in plate 1 indicate the base line simply.

CORRESPONDENCE.

Letter writing in short hand is no more interesting than it is helpful to the learner. You will naturally write more carefully when you expect that your letter will be read by some one at a distance; and this practice will in time give you a habit of accuracy. The perusal of the letters you receive will prove a most valuable drill in reading. You will be compelled to rely entirely upon the short-hand notes; whereas, in reading what you have previously written yourself, you are aided in a measure by memory It is a mistake to suppose that you must complete your course before undertaking such a correspondence. The better plan is to begin early, writing a mixed hand, that is, all the words stenographically that you are able, and the balance in long-hand Two points are to be guarded: 1st Do not put words that you have not learned into short hand. 2d. Do not fail to employ characters for all words that you have learned. The author, Prof Moran, will, within proper limits, furnish letters of introduction to all who make application.

LESSON I.

Line 12 By die Guy eyed bide gibe guide abide.

13 Beau dough ode bode Job goad obeyed doge.

14 Bay aid Abe jay gay jade guage babe.

15 Day age Joe go obey ago abode Dido.

First—Copy Plate 1 ten times. Use a fine pointed pen, black ink, and a good quality of ruled paper. Observe carefully the following points: Make the characters, or letters, all the same length, — rather short, not too long. Place them quite closely together, and do not get them crooked. Each stroke should rest precisely on the line. In L 7 (line 7) joined *b* extends below the line. The rule is that the *first downward letter should rest on the line*. *B, d,* and *j* are always struck downwards, and *g* to the right. Just as you write each letter speak its name aloud. Thus, while you are writing L 1, say *b, b, b,* and L 2, *d, d, d,* etc. The letter in L 4 is called *gay* instead of *g*. The letter *I* should be made sharp-pointed, and the two short lines composing it *light*, not *heavy*. (See L. 9). *I* is always so written as to point *straight down*. The letter *o* should be very short — only one-fourth the length of *d*. *O* is struck at a right angle with the letter beside which it is placed. For example, *o* in L 13 slants to the right in *beau*, to the left in *Job*, is horizontal in *dough*, and vertical in *go* (L 15). It is so written as to point directly *away* from the letter, or stem, near which it occurs. *B, d, j, g,* are consonants, and *I, o,* and *a,* vowels. The letters, or marks, which express consonants, are called *stems;* while the dots, dashes, and small angles are called *vowel signs*.

Plate 1.

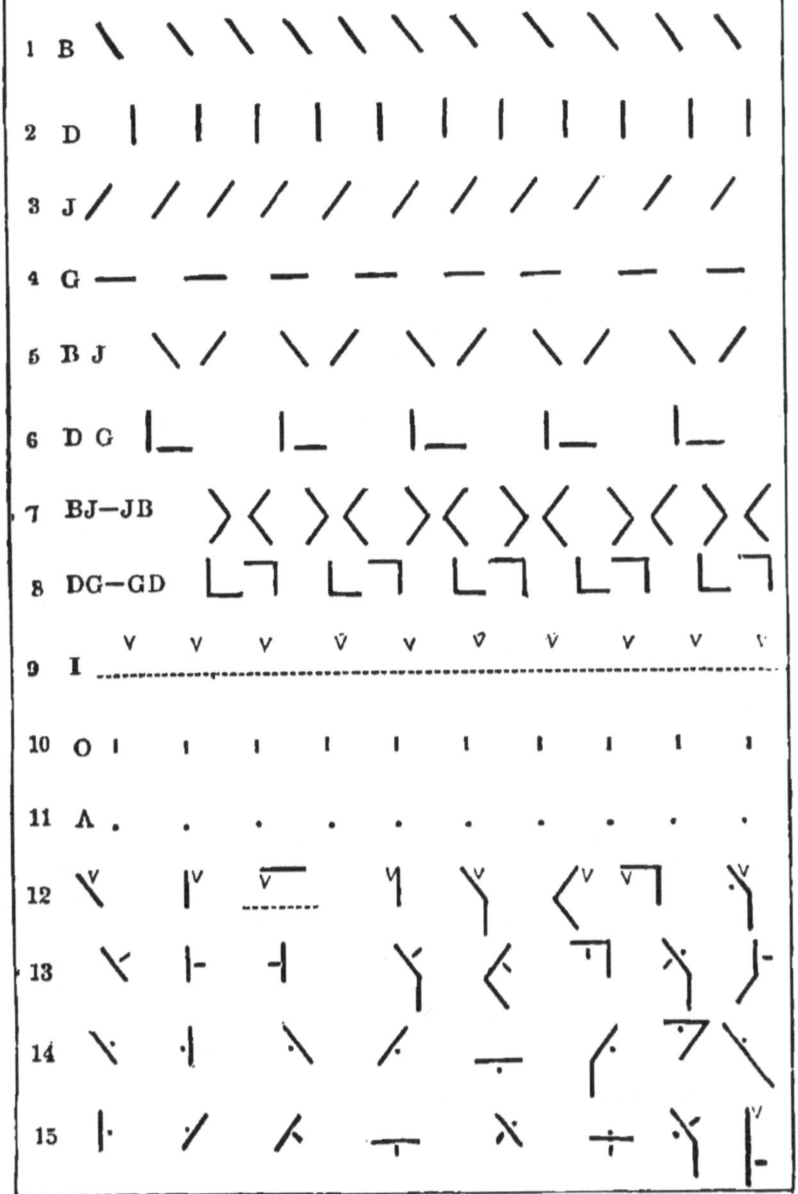

1 B

2 D

3 J

4 G

5 B J

6 D G

7 BJ—JB

8 DG—GD

9 I

10 O

11 A

12

13

14

15

LESSON II.

L 11 Tie dike Ike pipe pied tide chide typo.

12 Ope Coe oat poach code dope toto Tokay.

13 Pay ape ache Kate paid Jake Cato abate.

TRANSLATE LINES 14 AND 15.

First—Copy Plate 2 ten times. It is very important to make the light letters as thin and light as possible. The shaded strokes *b, d, j,* etc., should not be very heavy, enough so only for distinction. In writing any word, as *Jacket,* (*j-k-t,* *L 8*) do not lift the pen from the paper until the word is entirely finished. Be careful to write *t vertical.* It is a common error to slant it, making it appear like *ch.* The stem *ch,* L 3, is for convenience called *chay.*

Second—Frequently compare your work with the Plate, looking closely to see if it can be improved in any way. It should correspond as to *shading, straightness* of stems, and the nearness of the signs to each other. In *size,* the letters may be as small, and ought not to be much larger than those given in the Plate. The vowel dot *a* and dash *o* should always be placed at the middle of the stem. Write mostly with a pen; it is superior to a pencil in every way.

Third—Read one page of your writing without reference to the Key. Better still, read each page you write. L 5, for example would be read thus; *pe-chay, chay-pe,* etc. Short-hand is written by sound. Only as many letters are employed as there are distinct sounds heard; thus, *fo,* foe; *na,* nay; *lo,* low; *felo,* fellow; *do,* dough; *fabl,* fable; *fotograf,* photograph; *mikst,* mixed; *kwil,* quill. There are no silent letters, as *b* in *lamb.* Each letter is used only when its particular sound is heard; thus *p* is used in *pie,* but not in *sophist,* (spelt *sofist*). In *copper,* (pronounced *cop-er*) *p* occurs but once. Hence the usual manner of spelling a word has nothing whatever to do in determining the way to write it in short-hand.

Fourth—Practice on Plate 3 till you can copy it in two minutes.

Plate 2.

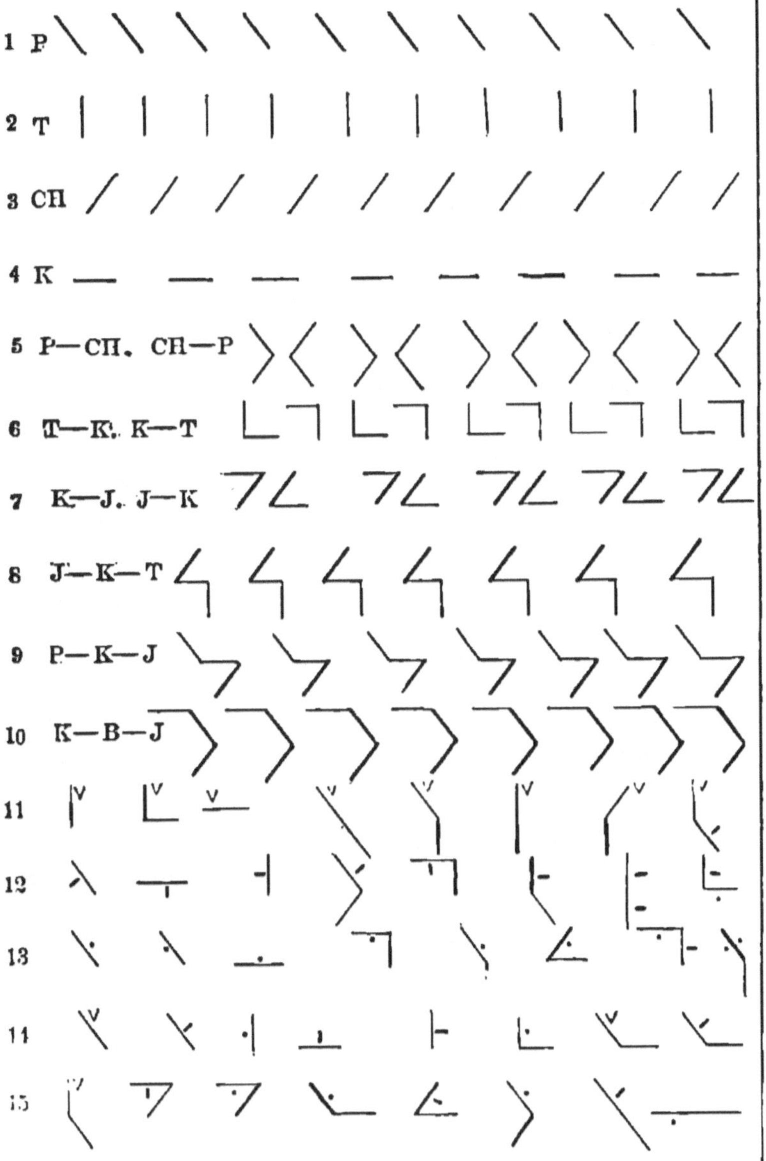

1 P

2 T

3 CH

4 K

5 P—CH. CH—P

6 T—K. K—T

7 K—J. J—K

8 J—K—T

9 P—K—J

10 K—B—J

11

12

13

14

15

ORAL EXERCISE.

Few vowels are written. Learn to spell by consonants, speaking the words aloud as you write them. Spend ten minutes a day upon exercises like the following:

T-k, take; b k, book; p-g (pronounced pee-gay), pig; b-g, big; d-ch (pronounced dee-chay), ditch; b-j, budge; j-b, job; t b, tub; k-j, cage; p-j, page; b-k-t, bucket; t-k-t, ticket; j-k-t, jacket; k-b j, cabbage; b-t-k, betake; b-j-t, budget; b-d-k, bedeck; j-j, judge; d-k-t, docket; k-m, came; t-m, time; n-m, name; j-m, gem; g-m, game; l-v, love; th-f, thief; h-v, heavy; m-v, move; sh-v, shave; m-m-k, mimic; k-m-k, comic; b-k-m, became; d-l-j, deluge; h-t-l, hotel; n-g-j, engage; s-k-p, escape; m-n th, month.

Beginners press the pen too hard upon the paper. That means more friction, more labor, more time, less speed. Touch the paper lightly. Make the thin stems as fine as possible; learn to dash them off rather quickly, barely touching your pen to the paper. Write compactly; that is, write small and place your words quite near each other. Avoid a sprawling style. Always carry in your pocket a short-hand sign book, manuscript, or exercise to read at leisure moments, while traveling, waiting for cars, steamboats, for lazy people to keep appointments, or whenever an opportunity for a few minutes' study may be had. Do not ask help in your translations.

CURIOUS ITEMS.

Some reporters can write four words a second for several minutes. Few speakers talk as fast as that. Stories are told of cases where the friction of the pencil, caused by its quick movement, would sometimes set the paper on fire. But these are only stories. In taking a short-hand report the pen really moves no faster than in writing common long-hand. The difference between the two is, that in short-hand a single brief character represents an entire word; sometimes several words.

Instances are related of cases where reporting was done under difficulties. One short-hand writer had to hold his note book against the wall and write standing. Another was obliged to write in the dark — had to " feel his way." It is so easy for some persons to report a speech, that they can do so while, to some extent, thinking of something else entirely; just as you can walk and talk at the same time. To the expert, indeed, short-hand writing is an easy task. We know a few lawyers, skilled in stenography, who are able, while addressing the court, to write down their remarks in short-hand just as they are delivered. They were able to write, speak and think all at the same time. This was not so difficult, however, as it appeared, because the hand kept pace with the tongue, and the tongue with the brain.

LESSON III.

Figures 1 and 2 show *direction* of letters, the rule being *toward the centre.* Fig. 3 shows their *attitude* and *relative length.*

3 Bee tea key gee eke peak peep deep.

4 Joy toy coy Boyd bough chow out outch.

5 Days goes pays pose chose gaze buys joys.

6 Side seat soap siege sage soak sake sate.

7 Spice space seeds sakes skies spokes spikes DeSoto.

8 Dow stow cows base chase scow peak cope.

9 Beach cheek keep keyed cowed gouge coke bestow.

10 Cages betakes beseech besiege beside decide outside decays.

11 *Word-Signs*—Common come give together which advantage is his as has.

12 I high how the a all two (or too) already before ought who. Translate Ls 13, 14, and 15.

EXPLANATION.

Vowels are written at the *beginning, middle,* and *end* of the stems, in what are called the *first, second,* and *third places.* The sound of a dot or dash depends on the *place* it occupies. A *third place* vowel, occuring between two stems, is put by the *second,* as *ow* in *cowed,* L 9. There are, likewise, three consonant positions; 1st, *above,* 2nd, *upon,* and 3rd, *through,* or *beneath* the line.

The circle *s* should be made small as possible, and always be placed on either the upper or right-hand side of the stem. If *s* begins a word, it is pronounced first, altho a vowel may be at the left of it. See *side,* L 6. Many of the commonest words are expressed by abbreviations, called word-signs. See Ls 11 and 12. These should be copied a great many times, and committed well to memory.

First—Copy Plate 3 ten times. Compare and correct.

Second—Write Ls 3 to 10 as the words are read to you from the Key. Carefully compare your writing with the plate, correct and continue writing until mistakes cease to be found.

Third—Practice on *word-signs* until you can write the list easily, forwards or backwards, as it is read to you. Practice on the Plate until you can write it in two minutes.

Plate 3.

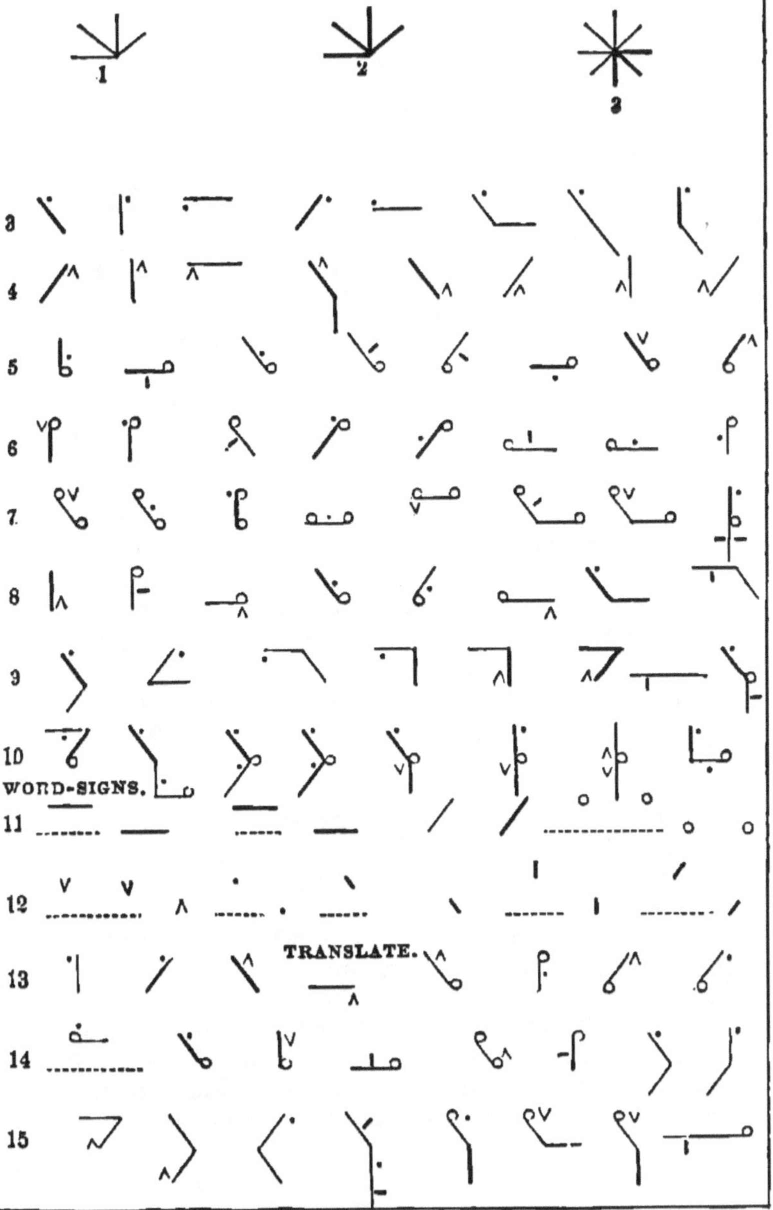

WORD-SIGNS.

TRANSLATE.

LESSON IV.

4 Fee fie vie lie lay lee mow (verb) mow (noun).

5 Oaf eve eel isle ire our life lower.

6 Nile knoll kneel name lope league chore boil.

7 Nose face sign save sore sown aims James.

8 Dio leech sours soils arise Fido voyage Milo.

9 *Word-Signs*—For have will me my him in any no.

10 Never now give anything that first we you.

Translate Ls 11 to 15. (The words in Ls 11 and 12 occur also in the exercise below.)

After *n*, *sk*, and in some other cases, *l* is written downwards. See L 6. It is then called *el;* and when struck upwards, *lay*. The signs for *I*, *oi*, and *ow*, should be made as small, light, and sharp-angled as possible. When two vowels are written by one stem, one is placed nearer, according to the order in which they occur. The circle *s* is always written on the *inside* of curves. At first, curves are difficult to write. As to degree of curvature, they should be nearly one-fourth of a circle. Be careful to bend them evenly throughout. In this and all remaining Lessons, spend at least two hours in copying and re-copying the Plate. Then write the words as they are read to you from the Key, compare with the Plate, and repeat until no errors are found. Also write and re-write the exercise a number of times. Occasionally transcribe your short-hand, and compare the translation with the original print. At first write *slowly*, and with *great care;* afterwards increase your speed gradually.

First—Practice on Plate 4 until you can copy it in two minutes.

Second—Spend twenty minutes writing the word-signs in Lessons III and IV as they are read to you miscellaneously.

Third—Write in short-hand the following Exercise:
Knee nay nigh know oil safe save file feel vale vile fame foam Lyle loaf loam Maine lief leave moil knife leak bore door fore pore pale pile peel bale bile fails toils vice.

Plate 4.

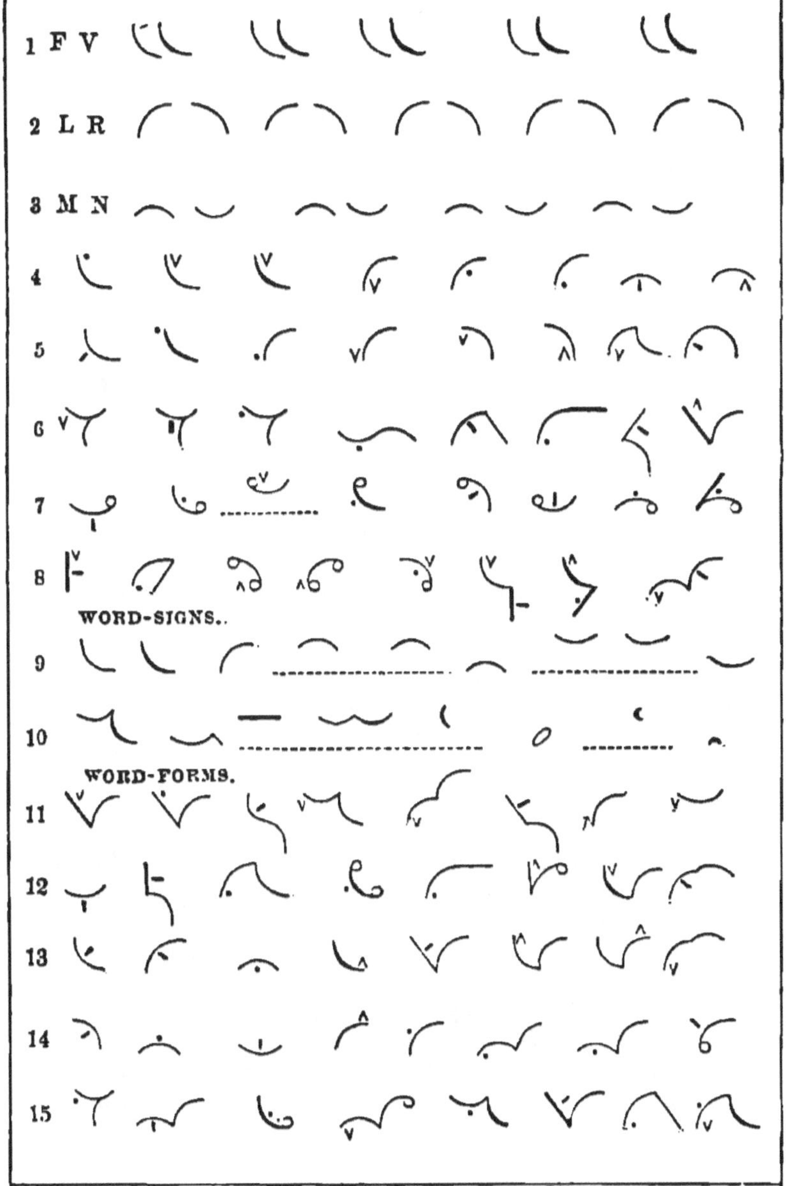

1 F V

2 L R

3 M N

4

5

6

7

8

WORD-SIGNS.

9

10

WORD-FORMS.

11

12

13

14

15

LESSON V.

7 Ace eyes thief loathe shave shire weak yoke.

8 Sew wrote rise row rout Reno rising roar.

9 Hoeing shaking heath shoal house hoax height yore.

10 Recede geyser Kaiser miser spacer chosen pacing fac-
ing.

11 This week I take my fifth lesson in stenography.

Word-signs. 12—Them [or they] think was your way he
are stenography advantage a and [or an] period.

Translate Ls 13, 14 and 15.

EXPLANATION.

In L 1 the *first* letter has the force of *th* in *three*, and is
called *ith;* the *second*, the force of *th* in *those*, and is called
the. When *s* has the sound of *z*, as in *was* or *goes*, it is
called *z*, and expressed by a thickened stem. *S* is most
commonly expressed by the circle; but the curve is needed
when an initial vowel precedes, as in *ace*, L 7, or a final
vowel follows, as in *sew*, L 8. In L 3 the first letter, called
ish, has the force of *sh* in *bishop*, or *ti* in *motion*. When
struck upwards it is called *shay*. The second, called *zhe*, is
equivalent to *s* in *pleasure*. The curves in L 4 are called
way and *yay*, and are the same as the consonants *w* and *y*.
H, always written *upwards*, is called *hay*, and *ng, ing*.
Shaded *m*, called *emp*, is equivalent to *mp* or *mb*, as in *temple*,
or *tumble*. Upward *r*, called *ray*, is used more than the
down-stroke. It is quicker, oftener secures a good angle,
and prevents word-forms from extending too far below
the line. When the circle *s* occurs between two straight
stems, it is placed *outside the angle*, as in *geyser*; at all other
times it is if possible placed *inside the curve*. The circle is
put on the left of up-strokes *hay* and *ray*.

Exercise—Moore hide rate heap road ride going reap
saw ease reach rake rose.

Sentences. 1. This boy's name is Jake, and he has a rake
by his side. 2. He will take the rope and go and tie the
cow. 3. This boy's name is James, and he has a spike
and a nail. 4. Milo will take them and file them for two
hours.

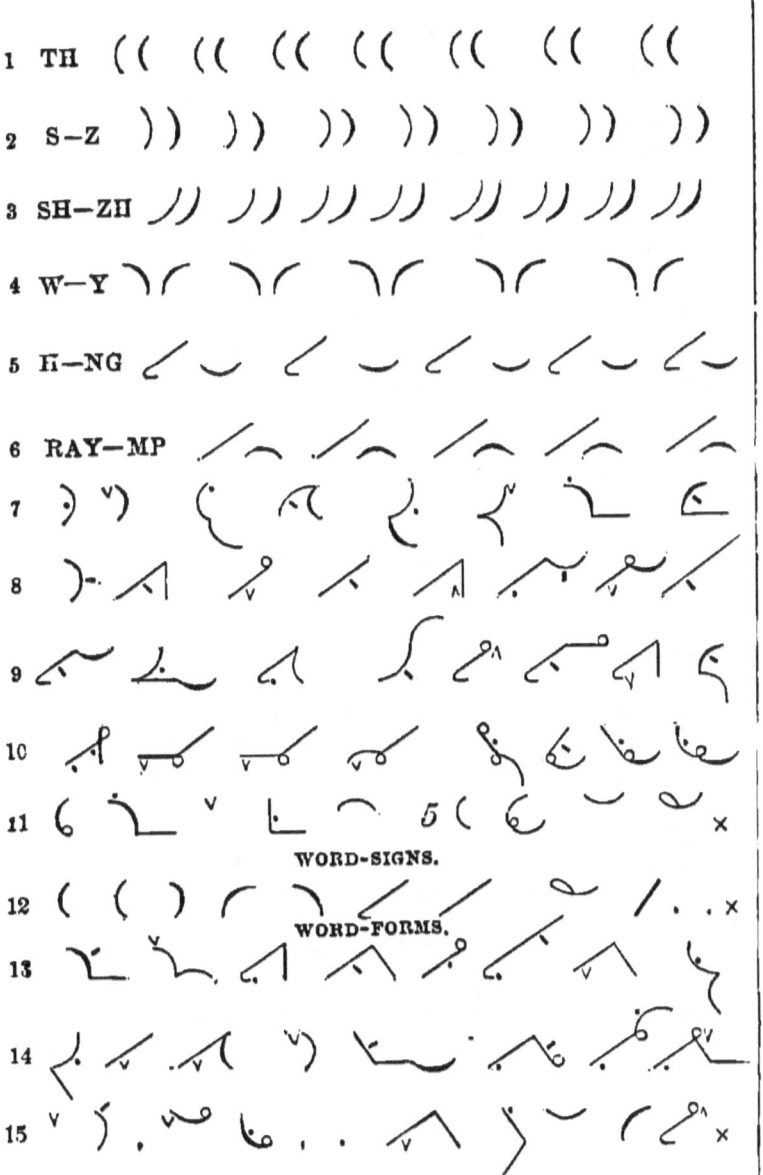

Plate 5.

1 TH

2 S—Z

3 SH—ZH

4 W—Y

5 H—NG

6 RAY—MP

7

8

9

10

11

WORD-SIGNS.

12

WORD-FORMS.

13

14

15

LESSON VI.

KEY TO PLATE 6.

1 Balk talk chalk sought arm palm boom loom.
2 Hoot gall shawl balm laws Ross yawl wasp.
3 Maul sauce gauze tomb far bar mar jar.
4 What will he do with that small jar of tar?
5 Paul will take it and pay for it right away.

Word-signs. 6—Of to or but on should with were what would. Translate Ls 7 to 15.

EXPLANATION.

The signs in L 6 should be as light and small as possible. *On* and *should* are always written *upwards.* The vowels, altho not commonly employed in reporting, should be thoroughly learned. The student will be aided in recollecting both the character and order of the long vowels by committing to memory the following rhyme:

In th-*e* g-*ay* c-*a*-r
S-*ee* gr-*ay* cz-*a*-r.
In sm-*a*-ll g-*o*-ld b-*oo*-ts,
T-*a*-ll d-*oe* sh-*oo*-ts.

Suggestions—Frequently review former lessons. Carry this paper in your pocket and devote spare moments to study. Correspond with two or three other students, using characters as far as you are able. If requested, the Author will furnish addresses. It is well to have a class-mate with whom to practice two evenings each week. Keep your diary in short-hand. Study a little every day—do not miss a single one.

Exercise—Saul fall tall laws tar Czar doom Paul ball pause cause also moss walk hawk snow geese goose sly toss small jaw thaw.

Sentences. 1. Do you know how to hoe peas? 2. He is going to show them how to peel a potato with a spade. 3. She likes to go to the lake and slide on the ice. 4. We have a loaf of rye and a bowl of ale for tea. 5. We also have a saucer of choice meal, and an eel which we will boil. 6. They have no rice, but oatmeal cake and a pail of spice beer.

Plate 6.

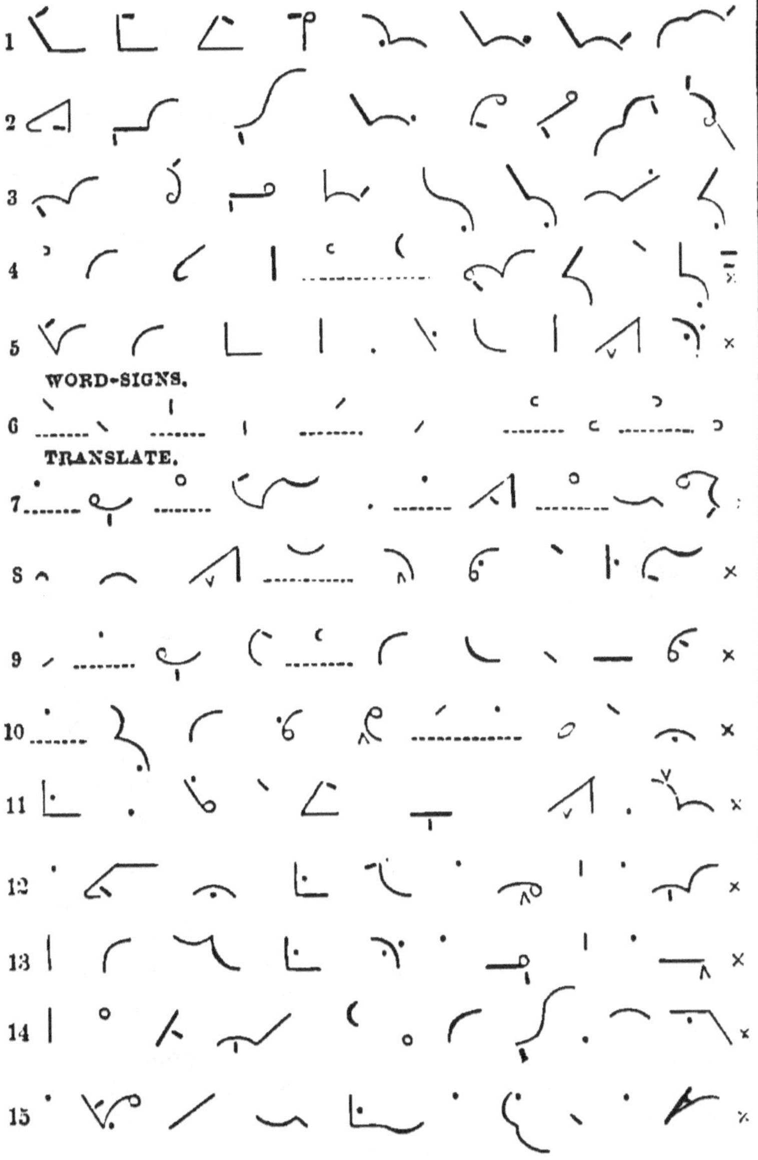

1

2

3

4

5

WORD-SIGNS.

6

TRANSLATE.

7

8

9

10

11

12

13

14

15

The student's chief concern is to know when to write and when not to write the vowel sounds. He can, however, be supplied with no specific rules. He must exercise his own judgment in applying the general rule, viz.: In reporting, insert as many vowels as may be strictly necessary to render the notes decipherable when the transcript is afterwards made. More vowels than these are superfluous, and ought not to be written. Just what, however, is meant by "easily decipherable?" Some persons require the notes to be fully vocalized, or they find themselves at sea when the report is to be written. There are some few writers who dispense with vowels entirely. They form their characters well, choose accurate outlines and bring to bear an exceptional judgment and memory in writing out their reports afterwards. Those who use vowels to quite an extent learn to depend upon them, and the practice becomes necessary mainly through force of habit.

Nothing short of experience will teach the young reporter just to what extent he ought to insert vowels to render his reports intelligible to himself. The difficulty he finds in reading certain outlines will cause him to vocalize them when next they occur. Gradually, also, he learns to drop vowels which he does not find helpful in transcribing. Stenographers in time acquire an intuitive faculty telling them as they write, no matter how swiftly, that this word or that requires a vowel, or else, in the peculiar connection in which it occurs, its meaning will be doubtful afterwards when the tracks of his flying pencil are being translated into "English."

The reporter, when pressed, writes larger than at other times. Some persons take this as an indication that a large hand is the most rapid. It proves just the contrary. The really skillful stenographer, when writing at high speed, is not flurried, and writes about as small a hand as usual.

There can be no question but that the greatest speed will be attained ultimately only by writing the characters near each other, cultivating a neat style, and writing as small a hand as practicable.

The first downward letter of any word should rest on the line. This is an important rule. To illustrate, in writing *cabbage* (in short-hand spelled k-b-j), *k* should be placed above the line so that *b*, the first downward letter, may rest upon it; *j*, the last letter, falls below the line. [See line 10, plate 2.]

The word-signs will bother you — they do everybody. They are hard to memorize; nevertheless copy them and keep on copying them until you know them as well as your a, b, c's. If not now, you will, in due time, thoroughly understand them. They are simple abbreviations like *Dec.* for *December*, *lb.* for *pound*, etc.

Please refer to the word *eke* in the third line of the plate. The vowel *e* is placed *above k*, because the sound *e* occurs before the sound of *k*. For this reason the sign for *ow* is written at the *left* of *t* in the word *out*, line 2. But in *key* and *toy*, the vowels come last, and the signs are placed *below* or on the *right side* of the consonant letters or stems. The second word in line 6 is *seat*. Here *s* is read first, then the vowel, and lastly the stem *t* is sounded.

Beginners make the *s* circle too large; there is no danger of getting it too small.

Make all letters the same length. This is easy. Keep this point in view while practicing, and you will soon form the habit of striking the letters of a uniform size.

Nine-tenths of all short-hand work consists in writing over and over many times a few hundred very common words; hence words and phrases which occur the oftenest must be learned the best. The reporter writes *him, is, will, I can, do not,* scores of times to *ocean, extracting, caliber, indigo, delve,* once. He will be sure to fail if he ever has to hesitate before writing one of the common words.

Quite likely all the letters look very much alike to you. Still they are all different. Let us see. Consonants differ as to form (straight and curved), shading (light and heavy), attitude (vertical, horizontal and slanting). Vowels differ from each other in these respects: They are, first, long or short; second, light or heavy; third, first, second or third place; fourth, dots, dashes or angles.

26

LESSON VII.

KEY TO PLATE 7.

1 Big beg bag bock buck book wife youth.
2 Itch edge egg ash ill Al at pack.
3 Mill inch niche knell fetch match snatch badge.
4 Cob knock lock rub tub rum took shook.
5 Wide wives twice few due new musty rusty.
6 Message judge waxen injure muscle deposit nothing earth.
7 Vessel citizen Mark agency hotel hasten maxim.
Word-signs. 8—Help notwithstanding New York City spoke special knowledge acknowledge several I (or eye).
Translate Ls 9 to 15.

EXPLANATION.

The short vowel signs are made very small and light.

Mnemonical rhymes: { Bill gets bat; { Lot cuts wood. Kills red rat. } Dot does good.

When a *second place* short vowel occurs between two stems, it is placed by the second. The rule briefly stated is: *2nd place long and all first place vowels, are put by the first stem, and all others by the second.* *Wi* is expressed by a small *right-angle*, and long *u* by a *semi-circle*. L 5. Proper names are indicated by a double underscore; as *Mark*, L 7. Common words are not usually vocalized. If a word contains two or more stems, it can usually be deciphered even if the vowels are omitted. See Ls 6 and 7.

Exercise—Write with vowels: Dick Jack pig Ditch dim Jim gem beck bell catch latch patch jam dam rob dock shock shop duck dumb chum gum thumb nook cook dusty valley. Without vowels: Desk cabbage picnic spell early bill many among live heavy damage enough Alabama Tuesday Sunday Saturday discuss this.

Sentences. 1. Amos has his bow in readiness. 2. He is waiting for the ducks to come up to the decoy. 3. Ed is too weak to make his way along the stony path up the slope.

Plate 7.

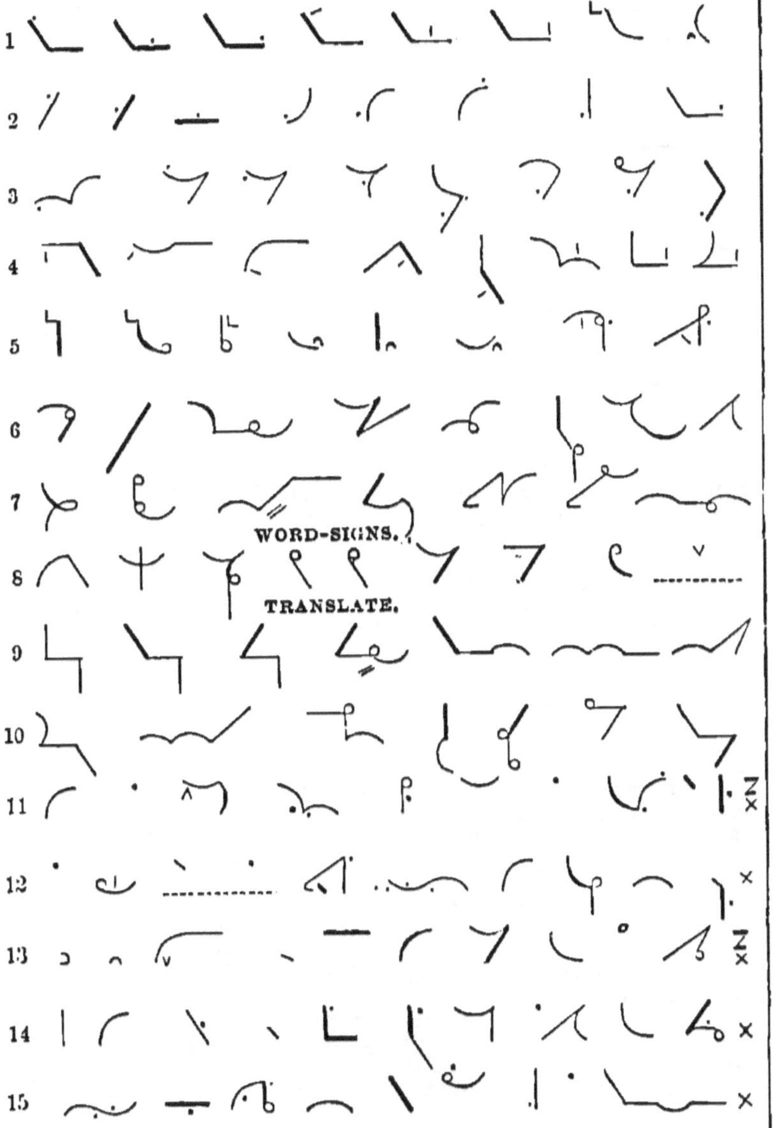

1

2

3

4

5

6

7

WORD-SIGNS.

8

TRANSLATE.

9

10

11

12

13

14

15

VOWEL TABLE.

The following table will aid the learner in remembering the *order* and the *place* of the six long, and also the six short vowels:

	LONG VOWELS.			SHORT VOWELS.		
	1st place	2d place	3d place	1st place	2d place	3d place
Dots................	Bee	Bay	Bah	Mit	Met	Mat
Dashes.............	Taw	Toe	Too	Cot	Cut	Foot
Dots................	Me	May	Ma	Pit	Pet	Pat
Dashes.............	Caw	Coe	Coo	Not	Nut	Soot

The words *a, an, and,* in phrasing, are denoted by a short tick written horizontally or vertically The tick selected should make an angle with the character to which it is attached. When not convenient to express these words by a tick, the dot signs should be used.

In the following exercise use *ray*, except where the downward *r* is indicated (by *ar*); when *l* is to be written downward it is so indicated (by *el*).

Write using *ray*: Ring road revive reveal (el) revenue ready repeal rash rate range wrong abhor birth bureau arrive earth march mark marry marriage memorial (el) merry admire memory mirror marrow notary period perish rare rarify injury theory thorough tornado variety victory hurry poetry Arizona arch burial.

Long vowels: Ate tea ace saw sea low oaf foe all ache gay aid dough awl ale lea ape Joe paw Joe shoe eve thaw jaw aim woe gnaw knee may Esau oar (ar) era (ar) ado age aught fee hay oat ode sew. (1st place) Cheek chalk heap heed tall leaf leap meal peal bawl beak bean beer hawk deal kneel (el) leak peach reap sheep team teeth wreath wreathe Neal (el) Paul. (2d place) Cake coach coal comb dale dame bail bowl cape joke fame gale game jail choke knave lame loaf nail (el) pole porch vale abate bore (ar) roam (ar).

Using dipthongs, write: Tie pipe vile knife mile defy boil coil foil row toy vouch Guy buy die chime couch coy dike fowl hide nigh owl foul pike pile rhyme shy sigh spike dye thigh tire toil annoy diet envoy royal Isaac sour.

EXERCISES.

S-circle junctions between two straight letters: Custody dispatch discuss dispose exhibit dispel gazet gospel justice succeed capacity Tuesday bestow disguise dusk gossip hostile receipt rest less upset restore custom task rustic risk.

Between a straight and a curved letter: Citizen desire desirous disarm dislike excel Harrison message music resolve instil musical pacific society specify answer dismiss visitor visit reason receive vivacity honesty Massachusetts Minnesota Erastus (ar) Missouri officer sarcasm (ar).

Between two curves: Innocence insanity mason scarcely Cincinnati refusal (el) license (el) offensive; (also write) sophomore sorrow genius science sublime Minneapolis.

Sentences:— 1. Your son is a wise youth, because he-seeks to-do-right. 2. In our city we-have some snow in-the-month of May. 3. Joseph Jackson, the-lawyer, has-a-large influence, and-he-may resign his office. 4. We-think of going into-a-business scheme together. 5. Our affairs are now in-such shape that-we may do-so if-we-wish. 6. Your absence in Alabama may restore your-health, and-thus be-the cause of-much happiness. 7. How-long-do-you think you-will reside in-the South? 8. I-will leave for Dakota in-the-month of March.

PHRASES.

As-he as-it-was do-so do-that do-they has-that have-also have-become have-long I-am-also I-am-ready I-became I-have I-know-that I-was in-any in-his in-it in-the-way in-them in-which in-your may-have may-never take-it take-that take-them it-was.

All-are all-his all-my all-right all-that all-the-way all-which all-you all-your and-have as-it-should before-his before-the before-you but-a but-may but-that but-the but-we for-a for-which has-a have-a of-that of-the-way in-the-way of-them on-that should-be should-do should-never should-they take-the to-him to-live to-love-them too-many who-may who-was.

All-such all-this be-said be-this before-this do-such do-this does-it does-that does-the does-this does-your for-such for-this has-this have-them have-such have-this how-may in-its-own is-this it-makes such-was to-his to-this which-has which-makes.

And-we as-it-should for-we have-we such-as that-you we-do we-have they-were we-were what-all what-do what-does with-the with-that would-say would-never how-you.

LESSON VIII.

1 Pump ample sympathy empire symbol thump lamp.
2 Cases paces necessary success faces loses causes.
3 Subsist exercise system Mississippi necessity races houses.
4 You-may do-you I-say-so shall-never you-will-never you-are have-time.
5 Does-it-make will-you-come how-long-have-you they-may shall-have we-have-no.
6 Will-you-take as-you-like it-is-so shall-I-have as-many-as as-long-as do-we-know.
7 I-was I-do-think I-have-no-time I-will-never I-write-you he-may he-would he-is he-has-no.
8 To-be may-be justice-of-the-peace as-well-as do-as-you have-his-name for-the-sake-of just-so.
9 Takes-us gives-us as-soon-as this-system makes-us United-States is-as as-is.
10 A-day a-space a-long a-common a-coil you-and-I he-and-you this-and-that.
11 The-advantage to-the of-the all-the for-the on-the should-the of-a to-a have-a.
Word-signs. 12—Important-ce improve-ment simple-ly impossible temperance December post-office become. Translate Ls 13, 14 and 15.

EXPLANATION.

The syllables *ces, cis, sis, ses, sez,* etc. are expressed by the large circle, about five times larger than the small *s.* Words grammatically related are usually joined together, providing the *phrases* thus formed are *angular,* and not *too long.* Words, when phrased, may be written out of their usual position. Observe 1st, only half the *I* is written, whichever *tick* makes the best angle; 2nd, *he* is the same as the last tick of *I,* excepting that it is *always struck downwards;* 3rd, *the* is precisely like either *he* or *I;* 4th, *a, an and* are expressed by a vertical or horizontal tick. See Ls 7 to 11. A hyphen between words indicates that they are to be joined together. Proper phrasing increases both speed and legibility.

Exercise—Camp lump damp pieces noses mazes noises scamp jump Texas Moses. Makes-time has-no-time for-a-long give-me it-is necessary I-think-you-will and-it-was and you-may-think a-desk the-bell. You-will always have time enough if-you-will but use your time to-advantage. Give to each thing no-time but-that-is necessary.

Plate 8.

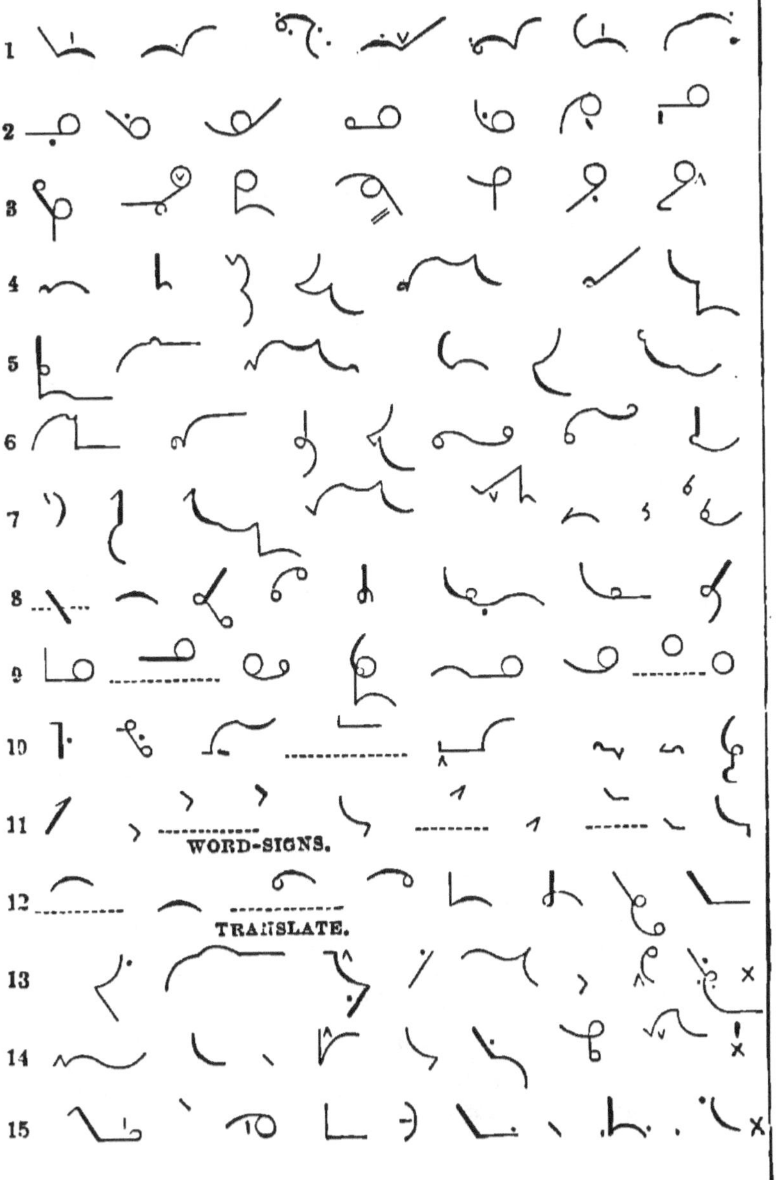

1

2

3

4

5

6

7

8

9

10

11

WORD-SIGNS.

12

TRANSLATE.

13

14

15

LESSON IX.

1 Play able evil civil fleeces shelf devil Majel.
2 Price breezes trump catcher glimmer trainer exaggerate distress.
3 Spry sober suffer over thrice pressure measure cigarette.
4 Puff spine above brain stiff strain cuff clown.
5 Flown thine assign ozone shine hen explain sustain.
6 Pines chance density lonesome extensive behavior reference sister.
Translate Ls 7 to 15.

EXPLANATION.

A small hook at the *beginning* and on the *circle side* of a stem, indicates that *l* is to be *added; eg. play, evil,* L 1. A hook on the opposite side indicates *r; eg. price, trump,* L 2. These hooked stems are called *double consonants.* A circle on the *r* side of straight letters implies *r;* see *spry, sober,* L 3. In order to bring the hook on the left side (to signify *r*), *f, v,* and *th* are reversed; see *over, thrice,* etc. L 3. A circle may be written within a hook. See *civil, distress, suffer.* When the r-hook is prefixed to *m,* or *n,* the stem is shaded; see *glimmer, trainer,* L 2. *R* and *l* are called initial hooks; the *f* and *n* hooks, which occur at the end of letters, are called final. *F* is attached to *straight stems* only, and is written on the circle side, as in *puff,* L 4. This hook is used for *v* also, as in *above.* The n-hook is put on the opposite side of straight letters, and is also attached to curves. See Ls 4 and 5. A circle written on the n-hook side of a straight letter at the end of words, implies *n; eg. pines, chance,* (but not *density*) L 6. All these hooks should be small and light.

Exercise—Black blame claim close globe pledge total gray grow break pray dray loiter pry trail cry drill keeper phrase favor Friday throw strike stray sprce sample cough crave bluff grove strive grieve pain stain bean bone dine twine taken turn bench lone mine fine abstain expense distance.

Sentences. 1. Every rose has its prickles. 2. Every path has its puddle. 3. Variety is the very spice of life. 4. For the upright there are no laws. 5. All cruelty springs from weakness. 6. Wise judges are we of each other.

Plate 9.

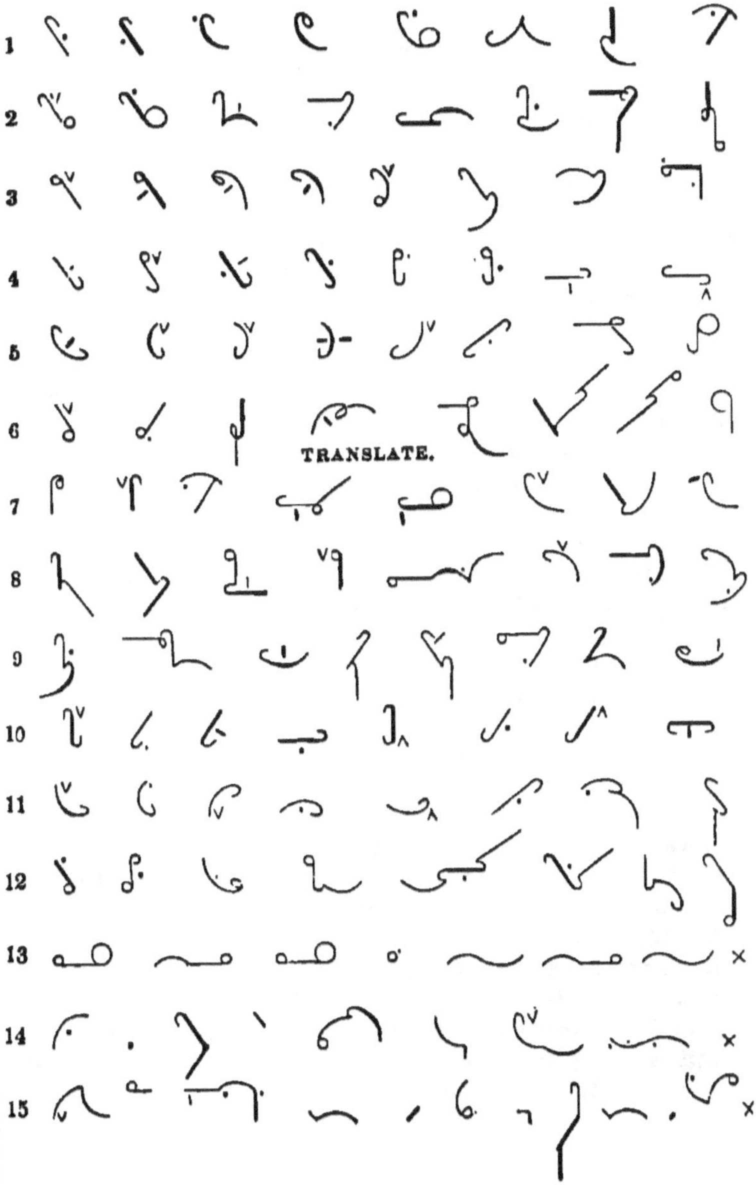

1

2

3

4

5

6

TRANSLATE.

7

8

9

10

11

12

13

14

15

TICKS.

Upward *r* and *ch* are never mistaken one for the other. *Ray*, as it is called, slants more and is longer than *chay*. Besides, it is always written upwards, while chay is invariably struck downwards.

In short-hand two or more common words are often written together, without the pen being lifted from the paper. The characters thus produced, which represents several words, are called *phrases*. The practice of phrasing increases speed, and is safe.

The sign for *I* is made up of two short ticks. In phrasing, only one of these ticks is written. That one should be selected which makes a sharp angle by joining to the next word. *He*, in phrasing, is also indicated by a tick just like the second tick of *I*, with this important difference, that he is always written downwards, while the second tick for *I* is struck upwards.

The six short vowels are indicated by a small light dot and dash written in the three vowel places. For example: A light dot, when written in the second place, has the force of *e* in *beg*, and a light dash the same power as *u* in *cup*. A light dash, first place, is equivalent to *o* in *job*. The learner will observe that the short vowel signs are quite small. This is necessary to render them easily distinguishable from the long.

Vowels trouble most students mainly because they are not well learned. But there are so few of them that a person can as easily become familiar with them as with the faces of his brothers and sisters.

Write, using short vowels: Ill kick lock rock chorus edge egg guess kiss haughty gem valley autumn daisy noisy espy ally alto dock chip chop cob dairy duck dumb Dutch essay gas gaudy hobby job lag lap pack lash latch lath leg lip luck mess mob odd pith rack shock Jesse Ella Emily Emma.

HOOKS.

The hooked consonants should be written with one stroke of the pen. By so doing, not only is speed increased, but the liability is lessened of forming the hook too large or too cramped.

The r-hook occurs mostly at the beginning of words; but sometimes it is to be written *medially*, that is in the middle of a word, as in *distress*, line 2. Here the circle is located on the left side of the stem, out of the usual position, in order that the hook may be prefixed to *t*. Strictly, however, it is not a hook, but an offset, which serves the same purpose.

The fact that either one of any pair of cognate or similar sounds may be represented by the same sign with no danger of ambiguity, has been fully shown in the case of the circle, which is sometimes used for *s* and sometimes for *z*, as sense may demand. This plan is safe, because *s* and *z* are similar sounds. So, also, are *f* and *v*. Hence, no uncertainty of meaning results from using a single hook to express both, as in the sentence, "They may well grv, considering their cause of grf." It is easy to determine here when the short-hand character *grf* should be read *grief*, and when *grieve*.

Ince this hook is attached to straight letters only, the stems *f* and *v* must be used whenever *f* or *v* are to be added to any curved letter. For example, *knave* is written with the stem *v*, for the reason that, according to the rule, the hook cannot be attached to the curve *n* to express the following *v*. *F*, like the circle *s*, is written on the left, not the right-hand side, of upstrokes. [See *behavior*, line 6.]

When a hook is joined at the end of the letter *m*, it is written *below*, that is on the *curved* side. It would be very awkward to write it on the upper side. It is different with *k*, to which it is easy to attach a hook both above and below. Hence, only one hook is placed at the end of curves, and this hook stands for *n*, because *n* occurs a good deal oftener than *f* and *v*.

LESSON X.

KEY TO PLATE 10.

- Learn color coral relate camel million tunnel analogy.
2 Hack hug hum hole hire whack Abraham mayhem.
3 Wall wore swine wine twin dwell quack Guinn.
4 Option passion station separation fashion physician compensation enslave.
5 Post coasting vest gazed against boaster fluster punster.
6 Letter order father weather cumber anchor.
7 Boat moat note gate plight died sobbed blade voted political.
8 Coats freights paint gift draft blend strained wend mend weld.
9 Mode send old sword middle needle failed poured attempt longed.
10 Core gall cull chart chill counterbalance circumstance selfish.
11 Complain introduce recommendation recognize castings yourself ourselves friendship.
12 Weed war woke wit web yield yoke youth Yeddo.
Translate Ls 13, 14 and 15.

EXPLANATION.

A large hook prefixed to r, m, and n, indicates l, and r when joined to l. L 1. A tick joined to k, g, l, r, m, or w, expresses h. When *hay* cannot well be written, a small dot is used. L 2. A small hook prefixed to l, r, m, or n, expresses w. A large w-hook is also used in the double consonants tw, dw, kw, and gw. See L 3. A large final hook indicates the syllables *sion*, *cion*, *tion*, *shion*, etc. When s precedes, this syllable is represented by a little curl on the opposite side. See L 4. This *curl*, when initial, stands for n, as in *enslave*. A narrow loop expresses st, and a broad one str. L 5. Doubling a curve adds tr, dr, or thr. L 6. Half-length stems add t, or d. See Ls 7, 8 and 9. Observe 1st, that t is not pronounced until all vowels and hooks which are appended to the stem have first been sounded; 2nd, that s, if final, is sounded *after* t; that l, r, m, and n, are shaded for d (L 9) except when a hook is attached. L 8. A vowel, to be read after a stem and before hook l or r, is struck through the stem, if a dash, or if a dot is changed to a small circle, *preceding* if a *long*, and *following* if a *short* vowel. L 10.

Learn also *Prefixes* and *Affixes*, (L 11), and *Coalescents*, L 12.

Plate 10.

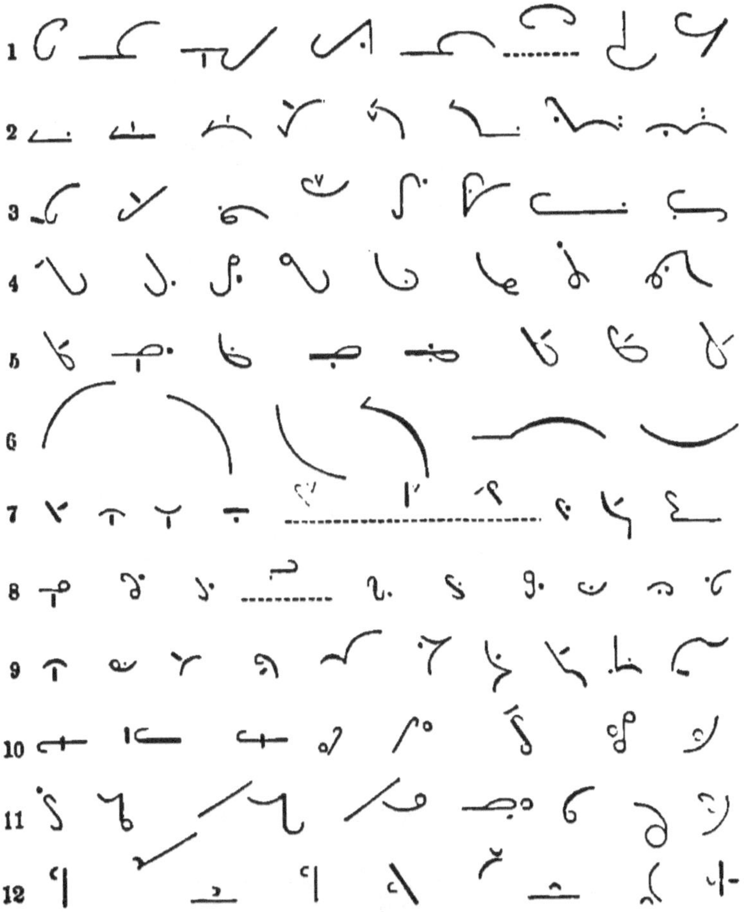

TRANSLATE.

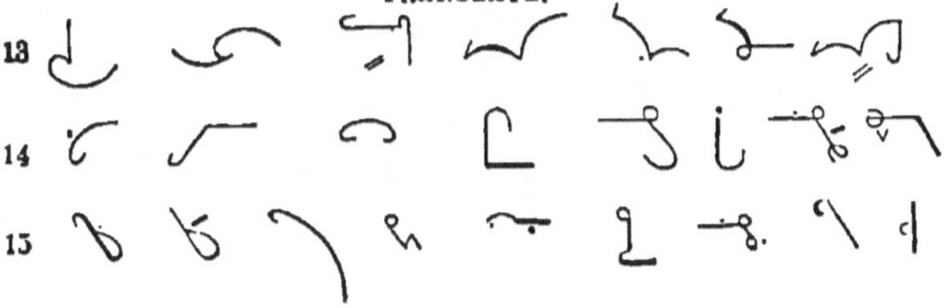

KEY TO PLATE.

1. Plenty chosen refrain profound candid sermon vixen splendid struggle. 2. Terminate willingly recover cannonade reduplicate calibre Brattleboro. 3. Exterminate troublesome excavate designate typographer octagon fantastic. 4. Freedom return detach dusty cheapen verify deeper branches manifold. 5. Extravagant occupant definite experiment monstrosity photographer chronology. 6. Bulk fork march forge milk forth birth roared. 7. Study stead stayed ousted bread bored birdie borrowed. 8. Worker purchaser digestive disturber refusal soldier laborer.

PHRASES. 9. Somewhere-else which-would-be which-would-make which-had-been which-has-just-been all-you-wish no-more-than-you can did-you-wish.

SENTENCES. 1. A-man's character is-the reality of himself; his reputation the-opinion others have-formed about-him; character resides in him, reputation in other people; that-is-the-substance, this-the shadow. 2. A-small leak will sink a-great ship. 3. A-fool may-make money, but it needs a wise-man to-spend it. 4. All is-not gained that-is put into-the purse. 5. Tell-your secret to-your-servant and-you make-him your-master. 6. If-you-would have a thing well done, do-it yourself.

EXERCISE.

1. Pain may-be-said to follow pleasure as-its shadow. 2. Peace is rarely denied to-the peaceful. 3. Pity is akin to-love. 4. Pity is love when grown into excess. 5. Prayer is to religion what thinking is to philosophy. 6. To-pray is to-make religion. 7. He-that-has-no cross deserves no crown. 8. The-Bible is-a window in-this prison of hope, through which we look into eternity. 9. Nothing speaks our grief so well as-to speak nothing. 10. Speaking much is-a sign of vanity. 11. The-soul knows no persons. 12. He who-is in evil is also in-the punishment of-evil. 13. The-rose is fair, but fairer we it deem, for-that sweet odor which doth in-it live. 14. Keep true to-the dreams of-thy-youth.

Plate

39

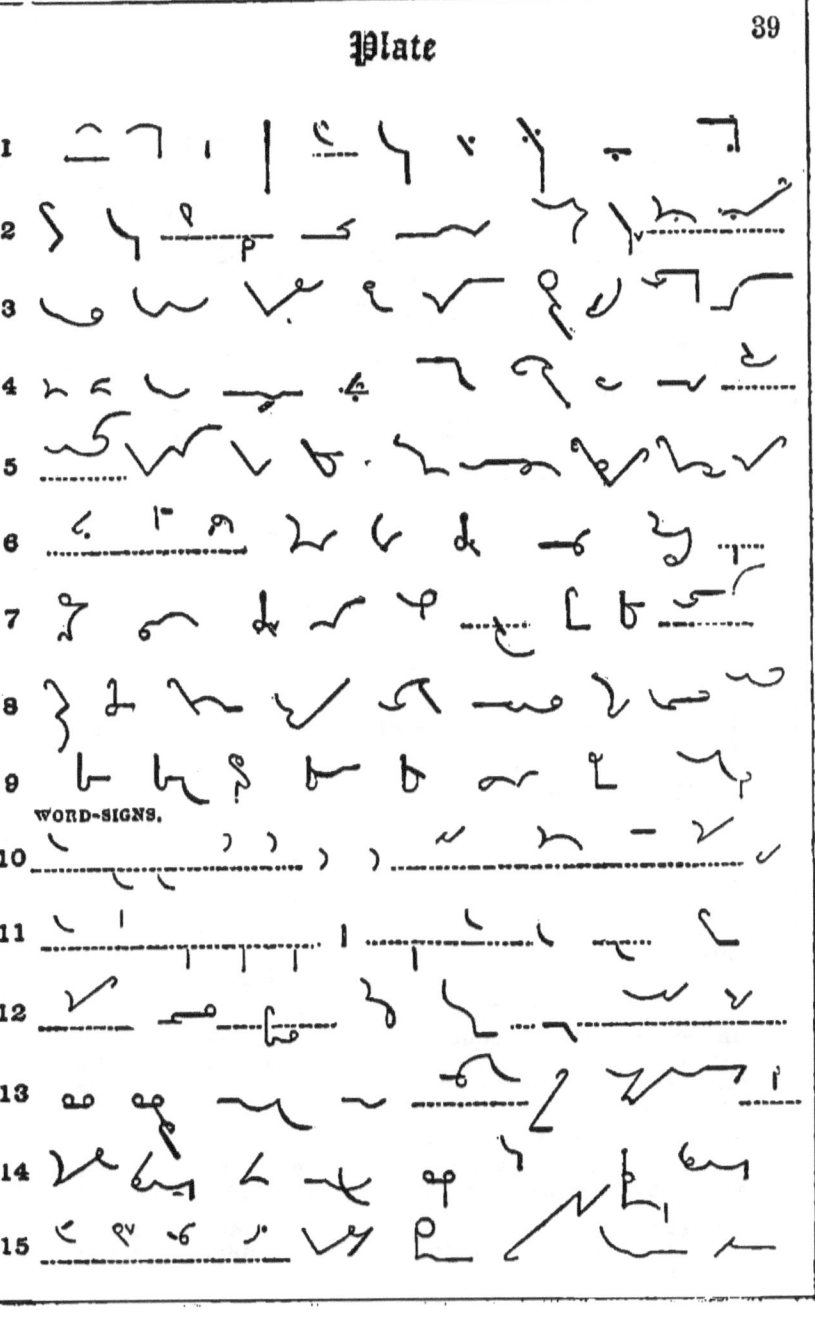

WORD-SIGNS.

PREFIXES.

The commonest prefixes and affixes are provided with brief signs, the greater number of which are joined to the main outline.

Con, com and *cog* are indicated by a dot, as in *compress, conduce, cognition.* Line 1. In most cases, however, this dot is entirely omitted with no loss of legibility.

Con, com, cog, when medial are expressed by separating the preceding from the following portion of the word, as in *accommodation, accompany,* etc., Line 4.

Counter, contra·i·o, are indicated by a slanting tick, as in *countermarch, contradiction, contribution,* Line 1.

Circum, self, are denoted by the s circle, as in *self-consciousness, circumvent,* Line 2.

Inter, intro, anti, ante, are denoted by the shortened *n,* joined to the remaining part of the word, as in *interview, introduce, antiseptic,* Line 2.

Magni, magna, may be indicated by the disjoined *m,* as in *magnify,* Line 2.

Mal, post, super, are commonly expressed as shown in *malcontent, postman, supervene,* Line 2.

KEY TO PLATE.

---

1. Compress conduce cognition accommodate recommend countermarch contradiction contribution. 2. Interview introduce antiseptic self-consciousness circumvent magnify mal-content postman supervene. 3. Commit commodity contemporary conquest community commentary confess compensate. 4. Accommodation accompany reconstruct recognition excommunicate incomprehensible conjunction inconsistent. 5. Counterbalance counterpart interpose interrogation internal interrupt antiquary discontent interest. 6. Commission compensation contempt command confidence composition constitute commencement conductor. Translate lines 7 to 10.

WORD SGNS. 11. Circumstantial malpractice construction constructive incompetent consequence consequent consequential. 12. Unconcern comprehend comprehensive antiquity antiquarian consider consideration reconsider confidential.

PHRASES. 13. For-a-consideration I-am-content in-his-opinion in-his-own-interest it-is-interesting under-any-circumstances every-circumstance that-conclusion.

SENTENCES. 1. Active natures are rarely melancholy. 2. Our actions are our-own, their consequences belong to Heaven. 3. Love is incompatible with fear.

Plate

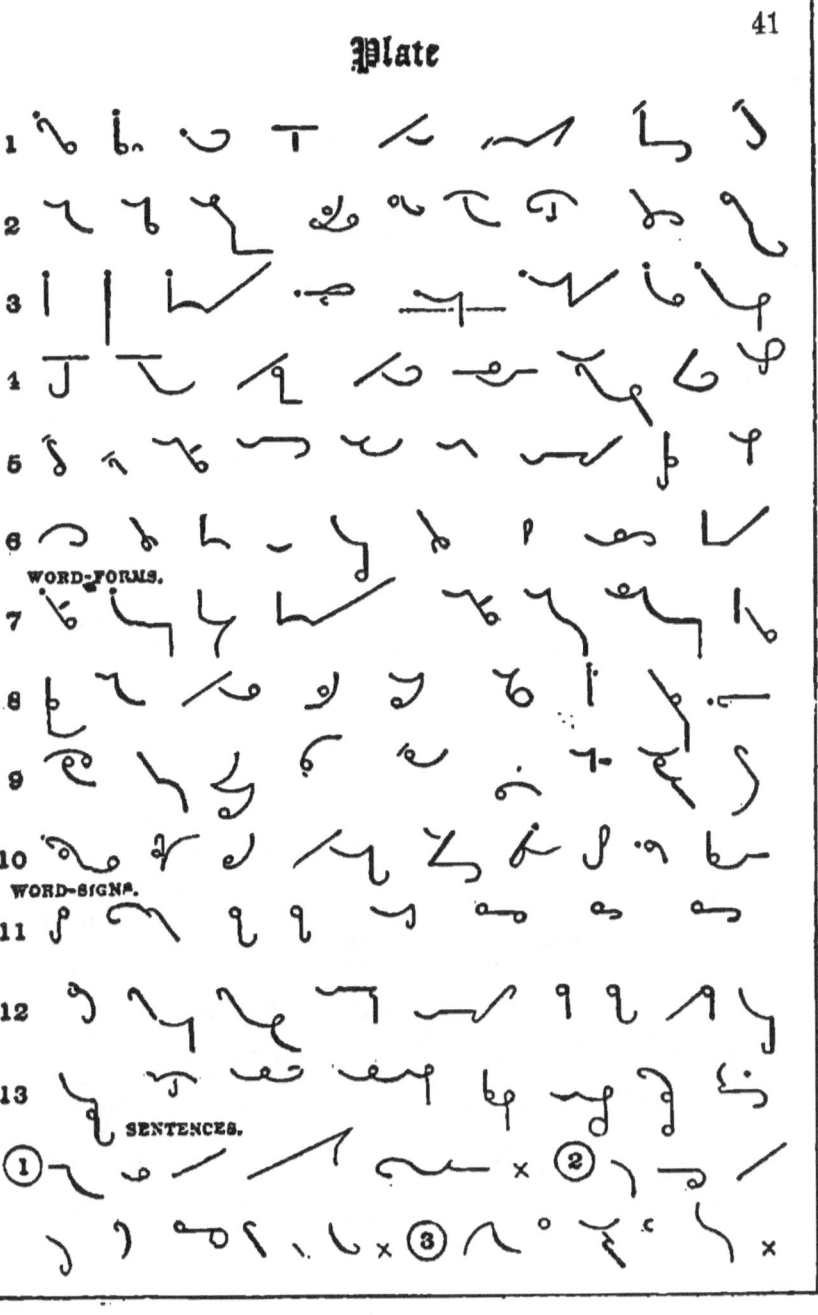

WORD-FORMS.

WORD-SIGNS.

SENTENCES.

AFFIXES.

List of affixes: *Ing ings ship ble bly ility ality arity self selves full hood soever ture ly.*

The *dot, circle* and *tick,* are used to denote *ing, ings* and *ing-the* respectively, in cases where the stem *ing* cannot conveniently be joined, as in *preserving, castings, doing-the,* Line 1.

The *s* and *sez circles* denote *self* and *selves,* as in *himself, ourselves.*

Ship is expressed by *sh,* as in *friendship.* But in order to avoid unsuitable outlines, *sh* is sometimes disjoined, as in *lordship, courtship.*

The endings, *ility, ality, arity,* are signified by the detachment of any letter from the preceding part of the word, as in *barbarity, fidelity, instrumentality,* Line 2.

The terminations, *ble, bly, ful,* are often indicated by *b* and *f* simply, as in *admissible, disgraceful,* Ls 3 and 4.

Mnt, when written separately from the preceding part of the word, indicates *mental,* as well as *mentality,* as in *instrumental,* Line 2.

Hood is denoted by *d,* usually joined, as in *womanhood.*

The ending, *soever,* is written *sv,* as in *whensoever,* Line 4.

Ture is expressed by *tr,* as in *structure,* Line 1.

KEY TO PLATE.

1. Preserving castings doing-the himself ourselves accountable lordship friendship graceful structure. 2. Fidelity individuality barbarity credulity hospitality formality instrumental legibility. 3. Vastly beastly regularity illegibility intellectuality womanhood disgraceful township courtship. 4. Whensoever ostensible citizenship engravings fixture manhood childhood admissible yourselves.

PHRASES. 5. Political-principles short-space-of-time as-little-as by-which-it-may-be by-which-it-would-be for-some-time if-it-is it-is-absolutely-necessary. 6. Let-us-be most-natural must-not-be present-question such-is-not-the-case this-is-not-the-case thought-we-were to-state.

SENTENCES. 1. No sensible-person ever made-an apology. 2. To-love-one that-is great is almost to-be great one's-self. 3. No man was ever so-much deceived by another as by himself. 4. Self-trust is-the essence of heroism.

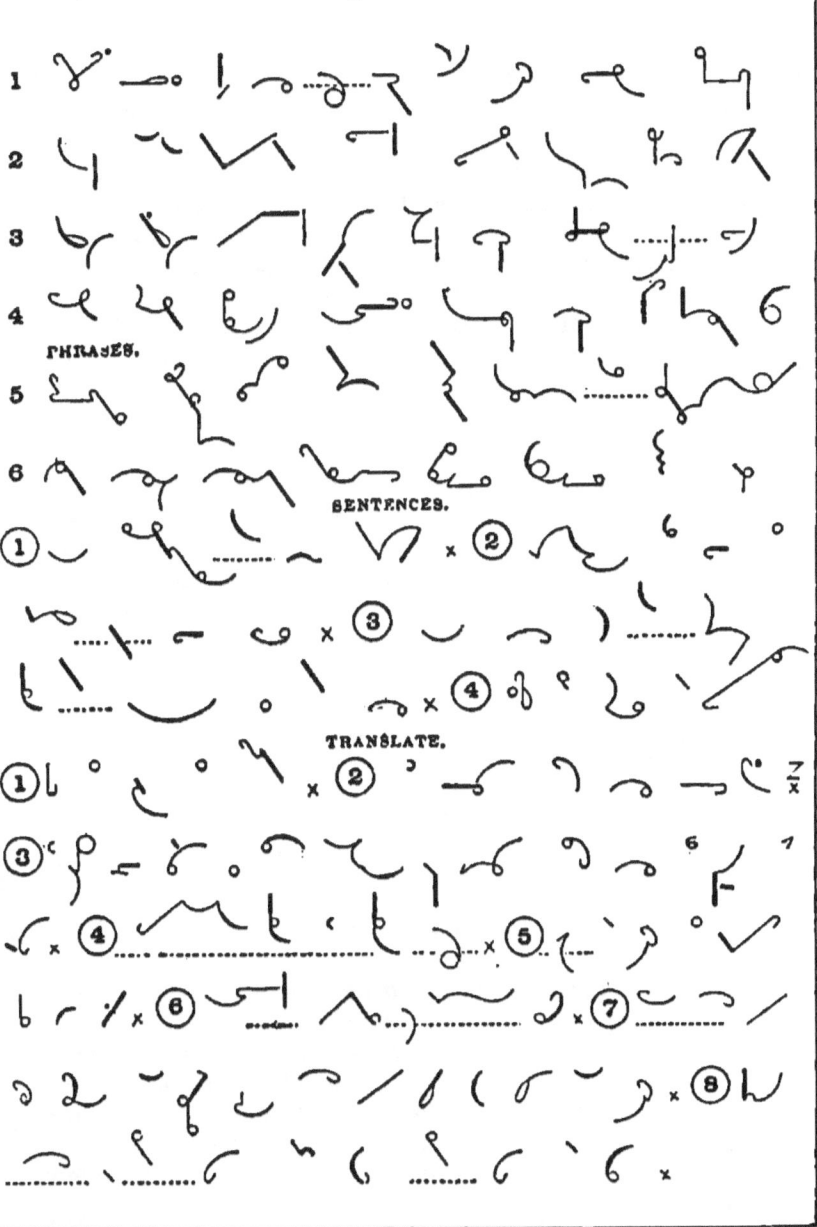

Plate

43

1

2

3

4

PHRASES.

5

6

SENTENCES.

① ② ③ ④

TRANSLATE.

① ② ③ ④ ⑤ ⑥ ⑦ ⑧

KEY TO PLATE.

Line 1. Might mighty date edit void avoid bate abate gate agate. 2. Obliged avoided stopped stood covered comrade infidel betide esteem immature. 3. Evidence fortune per cent swift rhetoric susceptible judicial integrity catalogue. 4. Estimate ultimate evident Connecticut adjudicate captivate multiply went acquired between. 5. Intentional perpetual apart abstract hermit antagonism Presbyterian prominent return. 6. Heat taught sort assimilate athlete dissipate exult ostentatious added. 7. Schedule seldom despite mutual necessitate beautiful delicate district integral. 8. Prejudice transact promulgate federal intolerable acquaintance wayward photograph intention. 9. Advocate defective splendid distinct distribute stimulate instruct invested.

WORD AND PHRASE SIGNS. 10. Feature future fact astonish astonishment establish establishment onward wisdom quite history world. 11. If-it it-ought it-would it-had at-it do-it had-it of-it have-it have-had people-of-God. 12. Historian Act-of-Congress at-all events east-and-west fear of-God good-and-bad in-the-world all-the-world.

PHRASES. 13. As-good-as as-good-as-possible could-never could-not God's-love church-of-God in-which-you-are-engaged what-did. 14. Was-received which-is-intended which-made could-nevertheless as-good-as-it if-it-did it-is admitted that-is-intended. Translate Line 15.

WRITING EXERCISE.

Bed could good shade stood decided comrade method instead evidence educated invade infidel.

In the following list both t and d are expressed by halving: 1 pos. east bottom got did light bid God meet invite might indeed fit knot lightning lot soft spot. Vocalize: Feat beat naught caught fought dot tight deed shot night slight naught sift feed knight neat salt sheet spite steed tide.

1

2

3

4

5

6

7

8

9

PHRASES.

SENTENCES.

①

②

③

④

⑤

⑥

LENGTHENING AND SHORTENING.

The writing of a curve double its usual length signifies the addition, first, of *thr*, second, *tr*, and third, *dr*. The writer's aim should be to write the lengthened curve more than twice its natural length, rather than less, in order to obviate any liability there may be to confound it with standard letters. For convenience long curves are named *fetter, vetter, thetter, metter*, etc. These in proportion to their length are bent much less than standard stems. To illustrate, *metter* extends but a trifle further above the line than *m*.

The lengthened *mp* adds *r* only, signifying *mpr* or *mbr*. Lengthened *ng* adds *kr* or *gr* only.

This principle is used to quite an extent in phrasing. Lengthening a curve adds *there, their* or *other*. Final *ng* is sometimes lengthened to add *there* or *their*.

One of the most useful contrivances in the entire system is that by which a letter, when shortened to half its usual length, is made to express an added *t* or *d*. Thus, *b*, when shortened in this manner is read *bt*, as in *bit*, or *bd* as in *bed*; *k* when halved, has the force of *kt*, as in *cut*, or *kd* as in *code*. *T* and *d* are the most frequently recurring consonants, and being cognates, or similar sounds, no ambiguity results from the expression of both by the same contrivance.

Learners are cautioned not to write the shortened letters more than half the usual, or standard length, else the two will become confounded. The practice of the writer should be rather to form these brief signs a trifle less than the standard length. To avoid confusion not only must the halved letters *not be too long*, but those of standard length also should *not be too short*.

Shortened curves are, in proportion to their length, bent somewhat more than full lengths; as an illustration it will be seen that *mt* extends almost as far above the line as *m*. This practice adds to the angularity of many word-forms.

When *t* or *d* is followed by a final vowel, it cannot be properly expressed by the halving principle; for if it were so indicated, it would be impossible so to place the final vowel that it would be read last. To illustrate *t* in might, may be expressed by shortened *m*; but the employment of the stem *t* in *mighty* indicates the fact of a following vowel.

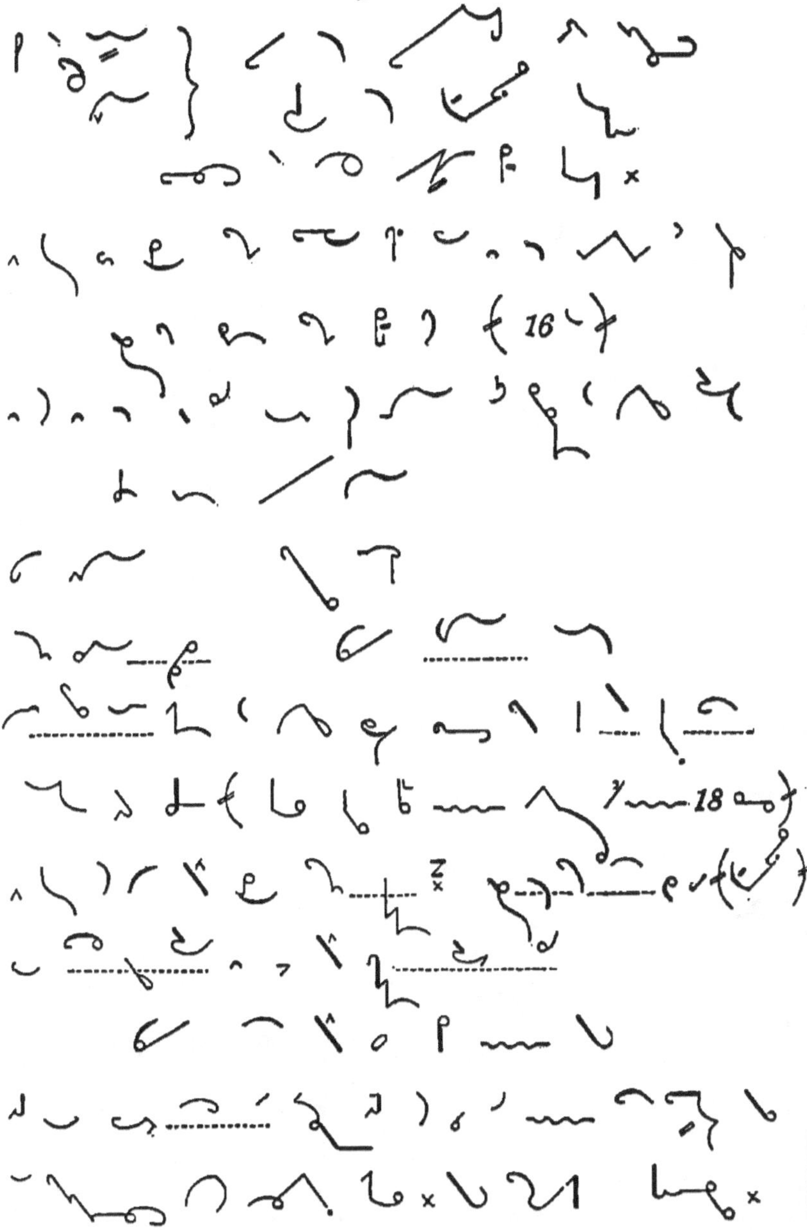
16
18

Plate

SENTENCES.

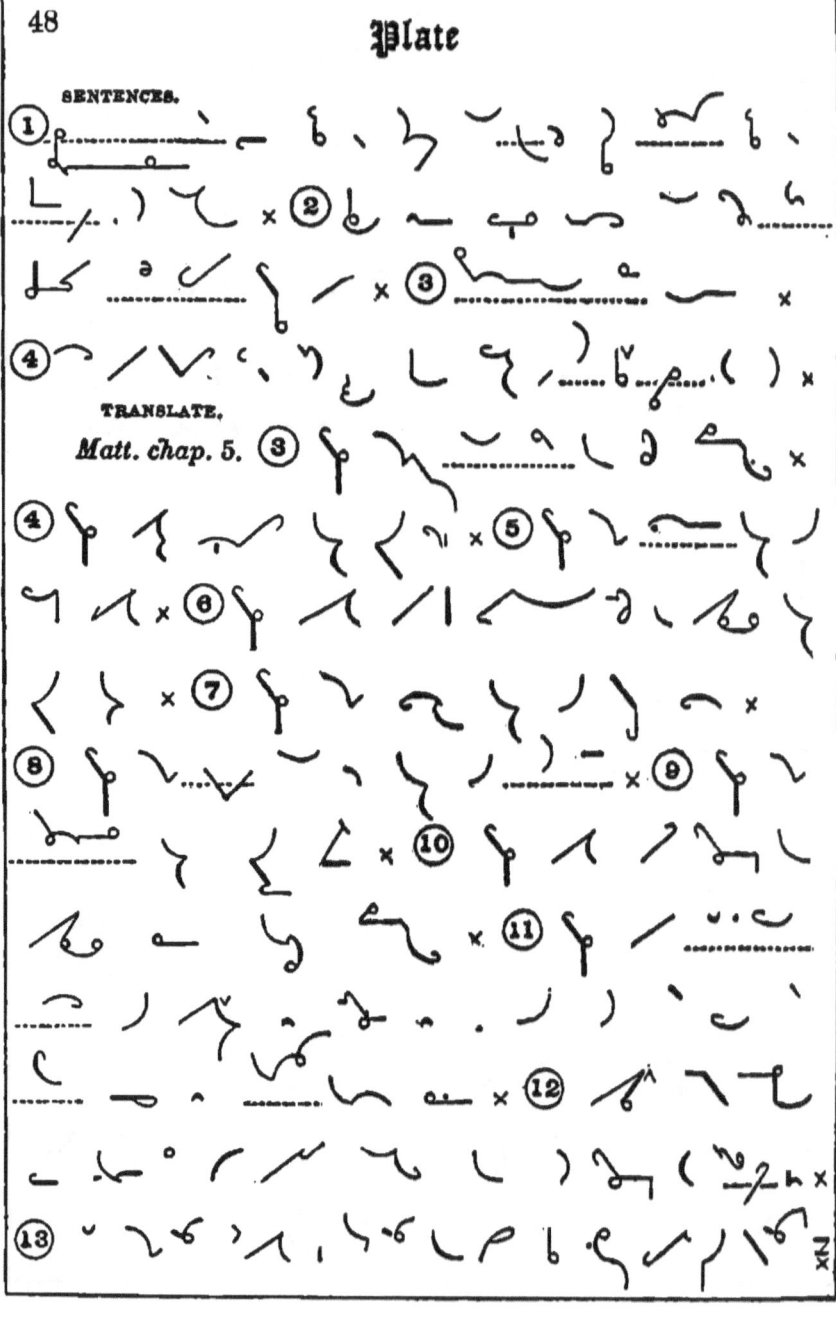

TRANSLATE.

Matt. chap. 5.

VOCABULARY.

A
Able-to
Able-to-give-it

Abundant
Accomplish
According

According-to
According-to-
his-contract
According-to-
the-instruction

Accuracy
Accurate
Acknowledge

Acquiesce
Acquit
Act-of-congress

Actual
Acute
Advantage

Advantageous
Advertise-ing
Advertisement

Affirmative
After
Afternoon

Afterward
Again-and-
again
Ago

Agriculture
All
Allow

Almighty
Almost
Almost-always

Already
All-the-world
Altogether

Always
Amanuensis
Ambiguity

Amendment
An
Analogy

And
Angel
Anguish

Anno Domini
(A. D.)
Annual
Antiquarian

Antiquity
Anxiety
Anyhow

Anything
Apostle
Appear

Appearance
Appeared
Applied

Apply
Appoint
Appointed

Appointment.
Appoints
Appreciate

Apprehend
Apprehensive
Approve

Are
Aristocrat
Arrange

Article
As
As-a-matter-of-
fact

As-fast-as
As-great-as
As-has

As-his
As-it
As-it-will

As-is
As-soon-as
Associate

Astonish
Astonishment
As-well

At
At-all
At-all-events

At-all-its
At-all-times
At-any-rate

At-first			Call	
At-it			Campaign	
At-length			Can-it	
At-once			Cannot	
Avenue			Can't	
Average			Capable	
Aware			Capital	
Awful			Care	
Awhile			Catholic	
Bank-note			Censure	
Baptist			Certain	
Barrier			Certificate	
Be			Certify	
Because			Challenge	
Become			Change-d	
Before			Chaplain	
Beforehand			Chapter	
Began			Character	
Begin			Characterize	
Begun			Characterizes	
Behalf			Child	
Behind			Children	
Behold			Christian	
Belief			Christianity	
Belong			Christianize	
Belonged			Circuit	
Beneficial			Circulate	
Benevolence			Circulation	
Benevolent			Circumstance	
Be-not			Circumstances	
Bequest			Collect	
Better-not			Collect-on-de-	
Better-than			livery (C.O.D.)	
			Collector	
Beyond			Come	
Bill-of-sale			Commercial	
Blunder			Common	
Board			Commonwealth	
Board-of-Trade			Communication	
Brilliancy			Company	
Brother			Comparative	
Brotherhood			Compliance	
But			Comprehend	
By-the-first			Comprehensive	
By-way-of-illus-			Concern	
tration			Confession	
Calculate				

Confidential Confidential-communication Congestion				Definition Degree Deliberate			
Congratulate Connection Conscientious				Deliberation Delight Delinquent			
Consequence Consequent Consequential				Deliver Deliverance Delivery			
Consider Consideration Consistent				Demonstration Demoralize Demoralization			
Consonant Constantly Constitution				Denominate Denomination Denominational			
Constitution-of-the-U.-S, Construct Construction				Denounce Dependent Derivative			
Constructive Continue Continued				Derive Describe Description			
Convenience Co-operate Correct				Descriptive Destiny Determination			
Correspond Countenance Counterbalance				Determine Develop Development			
Courageous Creature Criticise				Did-not Differ Difference			
Criticism Cross-examina-tion Cross-examine				Different Difficult Difficulty			
Cultivation Cure Danger				Dignity Disadvantage Disagree			
Dark Darken Darkness				Disappear Disconnect Dishonor			
Dare-not Day-of-the-week Dear				Dis-member-ed Dissatisfaction Dissatisfy			
Dear-sir December Defendant				Doctor Doctrine Do-it			

Dollar-s Domestic Dominion		Everlasting-life Every Every-one	
Do-not Downward Due		Evidence Examination Example	
During Dwarf Each		Excellence Excellent Exchange	
Each-are Each-will Each-will-have		Expect Expected Experience	
East-and-west Efficient Elaborate		Explanation Express Expression	
Electricity Eloquence Embezzle		Exquisite External Extinguish	
Emphatic Emphatically Enclosure		Extraordinary Eye Eye-sight	
Endeavor Endless Energy		Fact Failure Faithful	
English-language Enlarge Enterprise		Falsehood Familiar Fear-of-God	
Equal Equator Especially		Feature February Fellow-citizen	
Essentially Establish-ed Establishment		Fellow-creature Few Fewest	
Estate Estimated-cost Estimated-weight		Finally Finance Finish	
Estimation Et-cetera (etc.) Eternal		First First-class Five-or-six	
Eulogy Europe European		Follow For Foreign	
Ever Ever-and-ever Everlasting		Forever-and-ever For-instance For-it	

Forsake
For-the-first-
time
For-the-most-
part

For-the-sake-of
Forthwith
Fortunate

Forward
Four-or-five
Franklin

Frequent
From
From-first-to-
last

Full
Fundamental
Furniture

Future
Gave-it
Generation

Genial
Gentleman
Gentlemen

Give
Give-it
Given

Give-us
Glorious
Glory

Good
Good-and-bad
Govern

Government
Governor
Great·Britain

Greater-than
Great-extent
Guilt

Guilty
Gypsy
Had·

Had-it
Had-not
Half

Hand
Hand-in-hand
Handsome

Handwriting
Handy
Happen

Happiness
Happy
Hard

Hardware
Has
Has-his

Hath
Have
Have-had

Have-it
Have-not
Hazard

He
Health
Hear

Heard
Heart
Heathen

Heaven
Height
Held

Help
Hence
Herald

Herein
Heretofore
Hesitate

Hesitation
He-supposed
High

Higher
Highest
Highly

Highway
Him
His

His-is
Historian
History

Hold
Holiness
Holy

Home		
Honestly		
Honor		
Honorable		
Hope		
How		
However		
How-long		
Howsoever		
Human		
Human-life		
Human-nature		
Humor		
Hundred		
Humble		
I		
I-am-willing		
Idea		
If-it		
If-you-wish		
Illegible		
Imagine		
Imaginable		
I-may-be-there		
Imbecile		
Immediately		
Importance		
Important		
Impossibility		
Impossible		
Improve-d		
Improvement		
In		
Inaccurate		
In-as-many		
Inclination		
Income		
Incompetent		
Incomplete		
In-considera-tion		
Indefinite		
Independent		
In-describing		
Indicate		
Individual		

Individuality		
Indolence		
Indulge		
Industrious		
Industry		
Infinite		
Influence		
Influential		
Information		
Ingenious		
In-his-descrip-tion		
In-his-estima-tion		
In-his-experi-ence		
In-his-expres-sion		
In-his-life		
In-his-secret		
In-his-usual		
Initial		
In-order-that		
In-order-to		
In-point-of-fact		
Inquest		
In-regard-to		
In-reply-to		
In-response-to		
In-seeming		
Insignificance		
Insignificant		
In-some		
Instruction		
Instructive		
In-supposing		
Intellect		
Intelligence		
Intelligent		
Intelligible		
Intent		
Interchange		
Interfere		
Internal		
Interrogation		
In-the-first-place		
In-the-world		
In-this-city		
Intimacy		

Invention Investigate Investigation				Just-what Knowledge Ladies-and- gentlemen		
Iowa Irregular Irresistible				Landlord Language Languish		
Is Is-as Is-his				Large Larger Larger-than		
Is-it Island Is-said				Largest Lost-mail Laws-of-health		
Is-said-to-have Is-seen Is-such				Laws-of-life Lawyer Legible-y		
Issue It-had It-had-not				Liberty Liberty-of-the- people Liberty-of-the- press		
It-is-simply It-is-something It-is-sufficient				Lord-Jesus- Christ Loves-us Luxurious		
It-ought It-ought-not It-ought-to- have-had				Magazine Magnanimous Maintain		
Its It-will It-will-have				Majestic Majesty Majority		
It-will have-had It-will-not It-would				Malpractice Man Manager		
It-would-have- had It-would-not January				Manner Manuscript Marshall		
Jesus-Christ Joint-committee Journal				May-as-well May-be May-not		
Joyous Junior Just-as-certain				Measure Medium Member		
Just-as-much-as Just-as-well-as Just-been				Member-of-the- bar Member of-the- Legislature Memorandum		
Just-had Justice-of-the- Peace Just-say-so.				Men Merciful Mercy		

		New-York-City	
Mere		Next	
Messenger		Next-time	
Method			
Methodical-ly		Non-appear-	
Million		ance	
Minimum		Non-conductor	
		Nor	
Minister-ed			
Ministerial		North	
Ministry		North-America	
		North-eastern	
Minority			
Mistake		North-west	
Monarch		North-western	
		Notwithstand-	
Monthly-report		ing	
More			
More-or-less		November	
		Now	
More-than		Number	
Mortgage			
Most-important		Numerous-	
		questions	
Most-likely		Nutshell	
Mostly		Obedience	
Mr.			
		Obey	
Much		Object	
Much-are		Objection	
Much-quicker-			
than		Objective	
		Obvious	
Much-will		Occur	
Much-will-have			
Must-be		Occurrence	
		Of	
Must-expect		Official.	
Must-like			
Must-make		Oh	
		Ohio	
My instructions		On	
Myself			
Mystery		On-either-hand	
		One-of-the-most	
Natural-ly		One-of-the-best	
Nature			
Near		One-or-two	
		On-the-one-	
Neglect		hand	
Negligent		On-the-other-	
Negotiation		hand	
Neighborhood		Only	
Never		Onward	
Nevertheless		Opens	
Nevertheless-it-		Opinion	
is		Opportunity	
New-Hamp-		Or	
shire			
New York		Organize	
		Ornamental	
		Or-not	

Other Ought Ought-to-have		Practice Predominate Principal-ly	
Our-instruc- tions Our-own Ourselves		Principle Probability Probable	
Over-and-over- again Overwhelm Own		Problem Professor Proficiency	
Owner Paragraph Parlor		Proficient Profit Pronounce	
Part Partake Particular		Proper Property Prophet	
Particularly Particularize Party		Prosperity Protect Prove	
Peculiar Peculiarity Pennsylvania		Providential Public Publish-ed	
People People-of-God Perfection		Punishment Quantity Qualification	
Perform Perhaps Personal		Question Questionable Quick	
Phenomenon Philosopher Philosophy		Quiet Quite Railing	
Phonographic Phonography Pleasure		Railroad Railway Railway-car	
Political Popular Postage-stamp		Ransom Rather Rather-than	
Postal-card Posterity Postmark		Real Real estate Reality	
Post-master Post-office Postal-service		Recollect Recollection Recommend	
Poverty Practicable Practical		Recommenda- tion Reconsider Record	

Reduction Reference Reflection		Selfish Senior Sensation	
Reform Reformation Regular		Sentence Sentiment Set-forth	
Regularity Regulate Regulation		Set-off Seven-or-eight Several	
Relating-to-the-subject Reliable Reliance		Shall Shalt Shelf	
Religion Religious Rely		Short-hand Should Significance	
Remark Remarkable Remember		Significant Signification Similar	
Renounce Represent-ed Representation		Similarity Simple Simply	
Republic Requisite Respect		Singular Six-or-seven Slander	
Respectability Respectable Responsible		Some-one Something Sometime	
Revelation Revolution Roll		Somewhat South America South-eastern	
Romantic Rule Said-to-have		Speak Special Specially	
Salvation Satisfaction Satisfactory		Specialty Speech Spirit	
Satisfactory-manner Satisfactory-proof Satisfy-fied		Spiritual Spoke Spoken	
Savior Scorn Scripture		Square Squirrel Stability	
Season Secure Self-esteem		Statesman Stenographer Stenographic	

Stenography				There			
Stenographic-society				Therefore			
Stumble				There-would-not			
Subject				They			
Subjective				They-are			
Subsequent				They-are-not			
Such-are				They-will			
Such-are-not				This-is			
Such-a-one				This-has-never			
Such have				This-system			
Such-have-had				This-will			
Such-ought-to-have				Those			
Such-ought-to-hv-hd				Thou			
Such-were				Though			
Such-were-not				Three-or four			
Such-will				Throughout			
Such-would				Thus			
Sufficient				Till			
Suggestion				Till-it			
Suppress				To			
Supremacy				To-be			
Surprise				To-become			
Suspension				Together			
Systematic				Told			
Takes-us				Too			
Tavern				Toward			
Tedious				Towards			
Telegram				To-wit			
Tell				Transcript			
Tell-it				Treacherous			
Tell-us				True			
Temperament				Try-to-have			
Temperance				Tuition			
Temperate				Twelve			
Temporal				Twist			
Tendency				Two			
Termination				Two-or-three			
Territory				Unconcern			
Testament				Under			
Testimony				Undergone			
Thank				Uniform			
That				Union			
That-is-to-say				Unite			
The				United-States			
Them				Unity			

Universal		
Universe		
University		
Unless		
Unpracticed		
Unquestionable		
Unscriptural		
Unseasonable		
Unselfish		
Until		
Until-it		
Upon-his		
Upon-it		
Upward		
Us		
Use (noun)		
Use (verb)		
Usually		
Vacancy		
Value		
Very		
Very-well		
Virtue		
Washington		
Watch		
Water		
We		
We-always-like-to-have		
We-are		
We-are-not		
Welcome		
We-may		
We-may-be		
We-may-be-able-to		
We-must-be		
Were		
Western		
West-Virginia		
We-will		
We-will-not		
What		
Whatever		
When		
Whence		
Whenever		

When-it		
Whensoever		
Where		
Wheresoever		
Wherewith		
Whether		
Which		
Which-are		
Which-are-not		
Which-are-to-have		
Whichever		
Which-had-not		
Which-have-had		
Which-ought-to-have		
Which-ought-not		
Which-not		
Which-were-not		
Which-will-not		
Which-would-have-had		
While		
Whilst		
White		
Who		
Whoever		
Who-have		
Whole		
Wholesale-store		
Wholly		
Whom		
Whosoever		
Why-not		
Will		
Willingly		
Will-not		
Wilt		
Wisconsin		
Wisdom		
With		
Withdraw		
With-him		
Within		
Within-a-week-or-two		
With-me		
With-my		
Without		

With-reference-to		
With-regard-to		
With-respect-to		
With-whom		
Witness		
Woman		
Women		
Word		
Word-of-God		
Worker		
World		
Would		
Ye		
Year-s		
Yearly		
Yesterday		
Yet		
You		

Young		
Youngest		
Your		
Your-favor		
Yourself		
Yourselves		
Your-statement		
Yours-truly		
Youth		

APPENDIX.

Against		
Efficacy		
Perfect		
Mystery		
Manufacture		
Manufactory		
Right-hand		
Signify		
Yours-very-truly		

LESSON COUPON.

DETACH AND ENCLOSE IN YOUR LETTER.

GOOD FOR

ONE LESSON BY MAIL,

GIVEN BY

Prof. ELDON MORAN,

PRINCIPAL COLLEGE OF CORRESPONDENCE,

ST. LOUIS,   –   –   –   –   MO.

LESSON COUPON.

DETACH AND ENCLOSE IN YOUR LETTER.

GOOD FOR

ONE LESSON BY MAIL,

GIVEN BY

Prof. ELDON MORAN,

PRINCIPAL COLLEGE OF CORRESPONDENCE,

ST. LOUIS,   –   –   –   –   MO.

IMPORTANT STATEMENT.

The St. Louis, Mo., College of Correspondence is giving short-hand lessons by mail to more than four thousand students. More than one thousand of its graduates, who learned entirely by mail, are now holding lucrative situations.

Letter From a Practical Stenographer.

I learned entirely by mail, and served for one year as official court stenographer for the 15th District of Kansas. My speed is 190 words. I am perfectly familiar with the Moran copyrighted method of teaching by mail. A person who has not tried has no idea how clear and practical these lessons are. I will give further facts to any one who will write me personally. Address, 906 Bayard Ave., St. Louis, Mo.

HARRY E. DeGROFF.